E-Z DICKENS SUPERHERO BOOK THREE: RED ROOM

Cathy McGough

Stratford Living Publishing

WHAT READERS ARE SAYING

FIVE STARS - AMAZON REVIEWER

"This was such a fun story with so much going on. I loved the nature of the characters, especially EZ. It was really neat who his family was, and I simply adored the white room. In fact, I think I need my own white room and the new power EZ was granted toward the end of the book- I don't want to give away anything but, I mean how cool. As a gamer, I appreciated the plot a lot. In addition to the game I also thought the soul catchers were a very original and neat concept. That end!! Oh. My. I need to read the next part to see how things turn out."

Contents

Dedication	IX
Epigraph	XI
PROLOGUE	XIII
CHAPTER 1	1
CHAPTER 2	8
CHAPTER 3	10
CHAPTER 4	13
CHAPTER 5	17
CHAPTER 6	28
CHAPTER 7	46
CHAPTER 8	48
CHAPTER 9	51
CHAPTER 10	55
CHAPTER 11	58
CHAPTER 12	60

CHAPTER 13	66
CHAPTER 14	72
CHAPTER 15	76
CHAPTER 16	81
CHAPTER 17	83
CHAPTER 18	91
CHAPTER 19	104
CHAPTER 20	109
CHAPTER 21	115
CHAPTER 22	124
CHAPTER 23	144
CHAPTER 24	153
CHAPTER 25	159
CHAPTER 26	166
CHAPTER 27	169
CHAPTER 28	176
CHAPTER 29	188
CHAPTER 30	196
EPILOGUE	201
Thank you!	213
About The Author	215

For those who believe...

"A hero is an ordinary individual who find strength to persevere and endure in spite of overwhelming obstacles."

Christopher Reeve

PROLOGUE

TWO YEARS HAD PASSED, and it was December the first, E-Z's fifteenth birthday. Even though it was freezing cold outside, and snowflakes were blustering all around them, he and his family and friends were adamant about holding his party outside where they had a bonfire setup to keep them warm and a barbecue.

Now that Samantha and Sam were married, the Dickens' household was even more busy. There was never a dull moment when friends visited.

Sam and Samantha's wedding had been a small ceremony, held at the Registry Office. Lia had been Maid of Honour, E-Z was Best Man, and Alfred the Trumpeter Swan was the Ringbearer.

Lia had made fun of Alfred because he was dressed in a navy-blue bow tie and nothing else. Alfred wasn't flustered by this attention, since he knew he was in good company with others, such as former British Prime Ministers.

"If the great Winston Churchill thought a bow tie was good enough for him, then it's good enough for me!" Alfred said.

"He also smoked a big fat cigar!" E-Z said. "I sure hope you're not going to start smoking one of those too."

Lia sniggered.

"Steaks are ready!" Sam called. "If you like them rare come and get them now."

Only Samantha came forward with her plate at the ready. "Your son is craving rare today," she said, patting her belly.

"What my son wants, he gets," Sam said, lifting a steak onto his wife's plate. She poked the middle as her husband added a baked potato and a few strands of asparagus alongside of it.

Samantha munched on asparagus as she made her way over to the picnic table. She'd planned E-Z's birthday to a tee, and spent a lot of time decorating the table itself with Happy Birthday themed items. She sat down and cut her baked potato in half, then added sour cream, chives, butter, and a few shakes of salt.

E-Z, Lia, Alfred, PJ, and Arden stayed put because it was warmer near the firepit mostly. Uncle Sam didn't like people hovering about when he was manning the barbecue, so they stayed out of his way. Besides, they all liked their stakes well done and it also gave them an opportunity to chat on their own and catch up.

"What do you think of our Superhero website?" E-Z asked.

PJ and Arden looked at each other, then shrugged their shoulders.

"Come on," E-Z said. "What do you guys really think about it? I know you've had a look at the site, because Uncle Sam helped me look at the data. I had no idea we could find out so much information such as who is visiting our site, how long they are staying, what they are looking at. And I recognized your IP addresses. So, tell me what you think of it?"

"Whole truth? No holds barred?" PJ inquired.

"Brutal truth?" Arden added.

"Yes," E-Z coaxed. He lowered his voice to a whisper. "Uncle Sam did an excellent job. Still, we're not targeting to the right audience since we're hardly getting any traffic. Besides the two of you, and an IP address located in France we've hardly had any hits.

"A few people, like you they've come back and checked out the site a few times, but they don't stay for long. Uncle Sam suggested maybe we should start a newsletter, get people to sign up and send them updates but I don't know. Everyone is doing newsletters these days and it seems like a lot of work. Uncle Sam showed me he's signed up for about fifty of them!

"As to requests for help – which is the whole reason why we started up a website - so far all we've been asked to do were things local officials like police and the fire department handle. I don't like the idea of us rushing to save a cat up a tree, and having the fire department show up in full gear to do the same job. It's inefficient for them and for us. And it's embarrassing when they show up just as we're finishing up. Their time is valuable – they save lives every day. It feels disrespectful if you know what I mean? They are saving lives and are on call twenty-four seven.

"I think we need requests to be out of their realms, so, we're not wasting their time or making their jobs any more difficult than they already are. Sorry for such a long-winded speech, but, when I think of everything they did, after the accident with my parents…"

PJ and Arden leaned in close and whispered. They didn't want to hurt Sam's feelings – after all they weren't experts - or to take a chance he might overhear them and burn their steaks to a crisp.

"Uh, we totally get your point," PJ said. "Besides, the police and the firefighters are essential services, and they get paid to save people. Whereas you lot are volunteers."

"So, their website, and their online presence in social media is different than yours should be," Arden said. "And they have lots of staff, on many levels to maintain and keep everything updated."

"Whereas your site, needs something more superhero-ish – if that's even a word – and less Corporate. Like the legends, those in whose footsteps you follow. Look at some of the websites set up for them – and they are fictional characters. Imagine what we could do if we followed their lead," Arden said.

"Like what? I know you guys have some ideas, so share," E-Z said.

"Well, as you might have figured out, we did some brainstorming between the two of us. And we put together a staging website – it's not live and won't be until you approve it - of what your site could be like. It's on my phone. Look and see what we mean and think about the possibilities as this was done by us pretty quickly." PJ pushed start. The Three leaned in.

On the screen first were the words, "Welcome to the Superhero website of *The Three*." Then it zoomed in on E-Z in animated form. He was sitting in his wheelchair as one would expect, wearing a black t-shirt, blue jeans, and a pair of running shoes.

E-Z patted his hair down when he saw how bottlebrush-like the black streak down the middle of his blond hair looked. He never could get used to it.

"What's that, on my shirt, jeans and shoes? Is that a, logo? And how did you make me into a cartoon?"

"Yes, it is a logo. We thought the angel wing was cool and appropriate," Arden said.

"We used an app. to make you into a cartoon," PJ said. "We did some editing, on your arms. Hope we didn't go overboard."

E-Z's had a closer look as the animated version of himself crossed his arms. Now his rather more bulky forearms caught his attention and his cheeks flushed. He looked like a ponce, a poser. Did his friends really think he looked better like this? He cringed at the as E-Z on the screen's wings appeared. He hovered in the air, and pointed.

This was the first introduction to Lia. She arrived also in animated form. Lia was dressed from head to toe in a purple jumpsuit with a tutu. Her blond hair was up tight in a ponytail and over her eyes were a pair of purple sunglasses. She looked bouncy, friendly, and cute as she walked across the screen. She turned and stopped, like a model on a runway and struck a pose.

E-Z scoffed; he couldn't help himself.

"Well, at least I don't look like a poser with fake muscles!" she said.

E-Z didn't comment.

Animated Lia extended her arms forward, palms facing the ground. Then, voila, she turned them over. The left eye in her palm opened, followed by the right. In synchronicity they blinked. Lia held her pose, then whistled through her fingers.

"Wish I could do really that!" she said, trying to imitate the animated version of herself.

E-Z whistled.

"Show off," she said, elbowing him.

Now Little Dorrit came onto the screen. She was elegant and feminine, and as white as snow. The unicorn flew to Lia, landed, and dropped her head so the little girl could pet her. Lia hopped on, and Little Dorrit flew beside E-Z. They hovered, then turned their heads.

This was Alfred's cue. In cartoon form his bright orange beak seemed to glisten in the light. It was in direct contrast to his candy apple red bow tie. As he walked toward Lia and E-Z his webbed feet squelched like they were suction cups.

"My feet do not make that sound!" Alfred said.

"Uh, they do too," E-Z said with a smirk, as Alfred on screen spread his wings and flew to the side of his two comrades.

The Three posed. E-Z was in the middle facing with Lia to the left, Alfred to the right. Then it happened. *The Three* – well Lia and E-Z put their thumbs up. Alfred for his part did a wings up gesture.

"This is embarrassing," E-Z whispered to Alfred.

"No kidding!"

"Shhhh," Lia said as the voiceover on the screen kicked in. It was Arden's voice, but his tone was lower. He sounded like a game show host.

"If you need a superhero…E-Z, Lia, and Alfred – also known as *The Three* - are at your service twenty-four hours a day, seven days a week. Call ***-***-**** or send a message via social media.

When you need somebody to help you…Call *The Three*. They'll be there for you…immediately. You can count on them…because they're the best you'll see. Twenty-four-hours a day, seven days a week…satisfaction guaranteed."

"And now for the big finish," Arden said.

The Three folded their arms across their chests. Alfred folded his wings.

"Uh, that's not possible," Alfred said.

"Shhhh," Lia said.

Each with their chins thrust forward one after the other *The Three* struck a pose.

PJ hit pause.

"Taking into account what you said about jurisdictions, we might need to change this bit," he said. He pushed start.

"No job is too big or small for us!" A computerized version of E-Z's voice said.

Then a circle in the centre of the screen went round and round, like wi-fi trying to find a signal. Now the word BAM! filled the screen. Then the word SOCKO!

They watched as E-Z rescued a cat who was stuck high up in a tree.

"Oh brother," he said.

His animated character's voice continued.

"We're The Three

We're here for you!

Cat stuck in a tree...

We'll get him down for you!"

E-Z was shown handing the rescued cat to a family.

"Uh, that never happened," he said.

"We, uh, took a little poetic license," Arden admitted.

"We can fix anything you don't like," PJ said.

Now the circle appeared on the screen again, going round and round. When it stopped the screen was filled with the word BANG! Followed by the word ZIP!

On screen animated E-Z rescued a plane full of passengers. As he set the plane down, hundreds of waiting observers on the runway applauded.

"Now that's more like it," he said.

"Shhh," Lia said.

On screen E-Z said,

"Cause we're your friends!

Our services are free.

24/7

Cause we're *The Three!*"

Circle again, going round and round. Followed by BINGO! And BAM!

Now the roller-coaster rescue was recreated in animated form. It was very good. So accurate they could smell the candy floss and caramel corn.

"Oh!" E-Z said.

Lia applauded.

Alfred shook his neck from side to side like he'd recently been sprayed with very chilly water.

"I love it!" Lia said. "And thanks for including my favourite colour. How did you know?"

"I noticed, you wear it a lot," PJ said. His cheeks flushed. "I'm so glad you like it."

"What do you think, E-Z?" Arden asked.

Alfred glanced in E-Z's direction.

"That was uh," E-Z said, "uh...a good effort."

"Dinner's ready, come and get it!" Sam called.

"Let the birthday boy go first," Samantha said.

E-Z made his way across the yard, with Alfred.

"Talk about perfect timing," he said.

"Yeah, those two are still plonkers," Alfred replied.

"But their hearts are in the right place. It's a clever idea, just a little over the top for us."

"A little?" Alfred screeched.

"Okay, a lot, but they did give it a go. We can keep what we like and get rid of the rest."

When they all had their food, they sat at the picnic table and ate. The sky changed, and bright stars filled the heavens all around them. They ate their fill, then Samantha brought out the birthday cake she'd baked, and everyone sang "Happy Birthday!"

"Speech! Speech!" Arden chided and soon everyone joined in.

E-Z thought for a few seconds.

"Thanks for making my fifteenth-birthday special. I'd like to take a minute to remember my mom and my dad, and to share with you a birthday memory. If that's okay? I promise I won't get all soppy."

Everyone nodded.

Samantha who since she became pregnant was always soppy. Whether it be happy or sat tears, wiped one away before he'd even started. "I'm okay," she said, as Sam put his arm around her.

"It was on my fifth birthday. I didn't want a party, and asked to go and see movie instead. Instead of looking in the paper, to find out what was on we just decided to rock up and decide what to see on the spot. Either was they said I could choose as I was the Birthday Boy."

He closed his eyes for a second.

He was right back there at the theatre. There was Mom, all layered up in a parka. She had her earmuffs on, and she was rubbing her hands together the way she always did. Mom always wore gloves and complained her fingers got cold.

Dad had his knee length blue coat on over jeans. He didn't like to wear a hat into the city, because it would mess up his hair. His hands were mitten-less. Shoved into his coat pocket with his keys.

E-Z sniffed the air. He could smell the buttery popcorn inside the theatre, waiting for them to go in and order it.

They were looking at the posters.

"What about that one?" his mom said.

"No, E-Z prefers that one?" his dad said.

He opened his eyes again.

Instead of being in the backyard with his family and friends, he was back in the silo – again. He hadn't been back there since the archangels reneged on their agreement.

"Happy Birthday!" the voice in the wall exclaimed.

A panel opened in the wall beside him and out popped a cupcake. On the top it read, "Happy Birthday, E-Z." In the centre was a single candle already lit.

"Enjoy!" the voice said, dropping a knife and fork on the table beside him.

"Uh, thank you," he said. "Why am I here?"

"Wait time is four minutes," the annoying voice said. "Please remain seated."

Like he had any choice in the matter.

CHAPTER 1
BIRTHDAY INTERRUPTED

E-Z didn't touch the cupcake sitting in front of him, although it looked and smelled fine. He wondered what was going on back at his party. At least he knew they couldn't cut the cake until he blew out the candles and made a wish. Some birthday party back at home when he wasn't even there!

"Get me out of here!" he shouted. "I'm missing my own fifteenth birthday party and I was in the middle of telling a story."

The roof of the silo yawned open and Eriel soared toward him like a lightning bolt in a storm.

"It's good to see you again former protégé," he said.

"The feeling isn't mutual. Why am I here? I thought I was finished with the lot of you and it's my birthday – I need to get back to it."

"Yes, I do apologize for the timing – but we couldn't let your birthday pass without at least wishing you a good one."

"Uh, thanks, I think."

"And since you're here, why don't you partake in your birthday cupcake? And don't forget to make a wish – you'll need all the help you can get!" the archangel said with a snigger.

Besides E-Z a window opened, and a mechanical arm came out carrying a lit match. It set the wick alight, then retreated back into the wall so quickly that the match unlit itself.E-Z looked at the flickering candle. He wondered what that last comment meant but figured Eriel was winding him up. His brain went blank. He couldn't think of a single thing to wish for. Other than that, he was back at the house with his friends and family celebrating his birthday. As he blew out the candle, Eriel broke into song. It was a rip-roaring rendition of, "For he's a jolly good fellow, which nobody can deny."

"No offence," E-Z said, "But you're meant to sing Happy Birthday."

"It's the thought which counts," Eriel said. "Now that we've concluded the birthday segment of your visit, we'd like to know, have you solved the riddle yet?"

"Riddle? What riddle?"

"Yes, we suggested you try to make connections – in your past trials. Remember when we said we didn't want to spoon feed you? Any luck doing so?"

"Oh, it didn't seem like a priority or a riddle for me to solve, especially since you welched on your offer. But yes, I was writing in my notebook, making a record of things we've accomplished so far, and I did spot a couple of connections to gaming but they were purely coincidental."

"Coincidental! Definitely not. The incidents are connected – anyone can see that!" Eriel said, keeping his voice low so as not to lose his temper.

"Uh, sorry, but coincidences happen all the time. Do you know how many kids play computer games? I searched online. As of 2011 it said ninety-one percent of kids between the ages of two and seventeen play every single day. That's about sixty-four million kids worldwide."

'Ah, so you've zeroed in on it. That's good. Anything else you figured out about it? Or any concerns you might have? Any reason you should do more research – research is good. Initiative is very, very, good."

"No. I'm pretty busy, with other things – school and whatnot. Besides, if you want me to further pursue it – first you'll have to convince me it's anything more than a coincidence. I did check out a few more statistics. For example, there are more girl gamers than ever before. Many have created businesses on YouTube and are earning a living. Not kids of course, but from the stats I read online as of 2019 forty-six percent of gamers are girls."

Eriel tapped his long and boney finger on his chin, like he was pondering what E-Z had told him. "Ah, again I'm impressed. You don't find those stats worrisome?"

"Uh, no I don't." He inhaled deeply losing patience with missing his birthday. "Is it important we do this today? Can't you bring me back here another time? Nothing we're talking about sounds critical."

Eriel stopped tapping and his right eyebrow shot up. He glared the the birthday boy.

"Or is it?" E-Z inquired.

Eriel waited before responding. He wrapped his tongue around the words, like he was having trouble getting them out. His raised the pitch of his voice to soprano and said, "An-y-thin-g el-se a-bou-t tho-se t-wo in-ci-de-nts? An-y-thin-g to ca-use a-l-a-rm? To s-et a f-ire un-der you?"

E-Z wished Eriel would spell it out and get to the point. He didn't want to embarrass himself by stating the obvious or by being wrong.

"Raphael was right, you are kind of thick."

"Hey!" E-Z shouted. "If you need my help, you are going about getting it in a very strange way." He ran his finger through the icing on the cupcake and sucked his finger. It tasted good, like cotton candy. "Killing. One was trying to kill me, and the other was killing people in a store. Both said their motives were game related."

"Bull's eye," Eriel said.

"And?"

"Never mind!" Eriel disappeared through the ceiling, singing, "Thick as a brick, thick as a brick, thick as a brick."

E-Z raised his fists in the air. "You come back here and say that to my face!"

Eriel's laughter rang out, bouncing off the walls.

PFFT.

"Uh, thank you," E-Z said, then he found himself back home, at his party. Everyone was busy, playing games, doing their own thing – like he wasn't there at all – which he hadn't been.

He watched as Sam took his turn at ladder ball. He wasn't particularly good at this, but E-Z went over and watched his second attempt anyway. After he'd finished his toss, missing the target entirely he went to his nephew's side.

"I see you're still working on getting the hang of this game," E-Z said.

"Yes, it's an acquired talent. Where did you go by the way?"

"Eriel wanted to wish me a happy birthday, among other things."

"Uh, that was nice of him. Wasn't it?"

"Well, you know Eriel. He never does anything without a motive. In this case, he wanted me to make a connection based upon a memory."

"A memory of what? Your parents? The accident?":

"No, he wanted me to make a connection between two of the trial instigators. Which by the way I did. Then he left saying I was thick as a brick."

"How rude!" Lia exclaimed. She'd been listening in since she was bored silly by the ball throwing game.

"And on your birthday too," Alfred said. He was even more hopeless than Sam was since he had to toss the balls using his beak.

"Want to have a go?" PJ asked, handing the ball to E-Z who repositioned his chair in front of the target, then tossed the ball. It hit the upper rung, spun around a few times, and landed in the premium position.

"That's how you do it!" Sam said.

"PJ and I have been tossing throws like that throughout the game," Arden said.

"Ah, but you're not my nephew," Sam replied.

The party went on until it was too dark to play any more games, and everyone decided not to do a sing along. PJ and Arden made their way home while E-Z and the rest of the gang went to bed.

CHAPTER 2
TROUBLE

TWO DAYS AFTER E-Z's birthday party, PJ and Arden found themselves in a bit of bother.

It was Lia, who had a vision something was wrong. She recalled the vision to Alfred and E-Z, "It was like they were in a trance. And they were both sitting at their desks, staring at blank computer screens."

"Nothing unusual about that," E-Z said. "They do often play games together, and maybe they were asleep."

"With their eyes open?"

"Okay, let's go on over there," E-Z said.

"It's in the middle of the night!" Alfred exclaimed.

"Still, we better check it out."

The Three snuck out of the house, deciding to go to PJ's first as his was the closest.

"I don't think his parents are going to appreciate such a late visit," Alfred said.

"They'll understand," Lia said, as she rang the front doorbell.

Moments later, a very sleepy man, rubbing his eyes, threw open the door in his pajamas – PJ's father.

"Who is it?" his mother called from inside.

"It's PJ's friends," his father said. "Is anything wrong?"

"Uh," E-Z said, "Sorry to bother you but, we really need to see PJ. It's urgent."

"You'd better come in then," PJ's dad said.

CHAPTER 3

EARLIER

ARLIER IN THE EVENING, PJ and Arden had been working on the Superhero Website. They'd updated information, and added in a few new elements.

In the past when a request came through for assistance an email would be sent to the inbox. Next time anyone logged on, they'd see it and respond accordingly. With the new system, E-Z, Arden, and PJ would receive text messages instantly.

In addition to this, the person asking for request would receive a time stamped autoreply. PJ and Arden were certain this automated upgrade would increase confidence, and bring more traffic to the site.

PJ and Arden also setup a YouTube Channel with a Podcast. This was something new they'd come up with in a brainstorming session. They were excited to tell E-Z about it. It would be an excellent way to increase *The Three's* online presence. They also created a Community Board for open discussion.

The system also categorized incoming messages. For example, rescuing a cat from a tree. The Three had received multiple requests for this service. Since local officials were more equipped to answer this calls, PJ and Arden made it a Code Blue.

A Code Blue meant that by the time E-Z got there to rescue the cat, it had already been rescued. A Code Blue indicated he should wait, to see if the situation had been resolved before heading out.

A Code Yellow might be that someone forgot their keys or locked their keys inside their cars. Again, by the time E-Z got there, the situation had already been dealt with. Again, advice was to wait and check before heading out.

By categorizing Blues and Yellows, E-Z and his team would be able to focus on the more important calls, i.e., the Code Reds.

A Code Red was when lives or limbs were in jeopardy. Since the website was set up, The Three had received zero requests in this category.

Satisfied with how much they'd accomplished they decided to let off some steam. They joined a multiplayer game.

"Three girls," PJ typed to Arden.

"We can take them!" he replied.

The game began and at first, everything played out as it always did. They were thrashing the girls, going up level after level, killing everything in sight. Then suddenly everything came to a full stop.

CHAPTER 4

PJ'S PLACE

E-Z, LIA, ALFRED AND PJ's parents made their way down the corridor into his room. What they saw was mostly as Lia had envisioned. The difference was that the computer screen was still on. It was flashing and flickering while PJ appeared to be sound asleep.

"What's the matter with him?" PJ's mother inquired. "He should be in bed sleeping. Look at his posture. He's probably dehydrated. I'll get him a glass of water."

PJ's father moved across the room and shook his son's shoulders. He expected his son to wake up, but he didn't. Instead, he slid down in his chair, and would have fallen to the floor if his father hadn't have caught him. He carried his son and put him onto his bed.

PJ's mother returned, placed the water on the side table, then put her lips against her son's forehead. "No fever," she said.

PJ's father lifted his son's right eyelid and saw that only the whites of his eyes were visible. "Call 911," he exclaimed.

"No, I think we should call our family doctor, Doctor Flannel," PJ's mother said. "He's come here before for a home visit. When it's been an emergency – and this is definitely an emergency."

"Mrs. Handle," E-Z said, "He's going to be okay."

"Of course, he will," she replied, as Mr. Handle went out of the room to call Doctor Flannel."

When he returned, they all waited together silently, watching PJ as he slept. Like they expected him to jump up and start goofing off. It would be just like him to be playing up. Fooling them.

Mr. Handle was fidgety, bouncing his leg up and down while he sat. He stood, moved across the room, and bend down to look at the hard drive. He raised his foot, like he was going to kick it, but at the last minute changed his mind and pulled the cord out of the socket.

They looked on, as Mr. Handle began to shake throughout his body, until he dropped the plug. He turned and walked toward them. Behind him smoke poured out of the hard drive. Seconds later the monitor screen cracked.

"Grab the fire extinguisher!" Alfred called, but E-Z had already grabbed the glass of water and tossed it onto the box. It sizzled and joined the screen both absolutely dead.

PJ's mother ran to her husband, and helped him to sit down. "The doctor can have a look at you too when he arrives," she said. "You're so lucky. I can't handle the two of you being hurt."

"I'm fine," Mr. Handle said.

But to The Three he didn't look fine. He was pale, a little green and a little gray.

"Don't fuss," Mr. Handle said. "Thanks for the quick thinking, E-Z." Then to his wife, "Good thing you brought in that water."

"PJ will be very cross when he sees his computer is ruined."

"Now, now," Mr. Handle said. "He'll understand."

He was clearly filling better, as The Three noticed his breathing was back to normal, as was he pallor.

Since everything seemed in order, E-Z mentioned Arden. "While you wait for the doctor, we really need to check on Arden. We think he might be in a similar condition."

"They often play games together, but what on earth could have caused this?" Mr. Handle inquired.

"I don't know, but do you mind if I go and check on Arden?"

"You go ahead," Mrs. Handle said.

"Lia will stay here with you," E-Z said. "She can keep us posted, and if you need us, we'll come right back."

"Thank you, E-Z, and Alfred," Mr. Handle said, as he escorted them to the front door.

CHAPTER 5

ARDEN'S PLACE

E-Z AND ALFRED MADE their way to Arden's place. Before they even had the chance to knock, Arden's father Mr. Lester opened the door.

"How did you know?" he asked.

E-Z couldn't tell him the truth. So instead, he improvised a lie. "Uh, I've been best friends with Arden all my life, so I kind of know when something is wrong. Can I see him?"

"Sure, come on into his room," Arden's mother Mrs. Lester said. "Don't be alarmed. He's only sleeping. He'll be fine in the morning."

Mr. Lester took his wife's hand and led her down the hallway to where Arden was sound asleep.

"Oh," Alfred exclaimed, when he saw him. "He looks like he's in shock."

"Look under his eyelids," Mr. Lester said.

E-Z pulled his friend's eyelid back. PJ's pupil was visible, but it was bigger and looked like it might explode out of his eye socket at any moment. He closed the eyelid over it again.

Alfred Hoo-hoo'd. That's what the Lesters heard. What he said was, "What the heck would cause that? Fear? Or something more serious like a seizure?"

E-Z shrugged without answering. The Lesters were frightened and stressed out enough already, plus all they'd be doing is guessing.

"Where exactly did you find him?" E-Z asked.

"He was sitting in front of his computer," Mrs. Lester said.

"Was the screen on?" he asked.

"Yes, it was," Mr. Lester said. "We've put a call into our family doctor. He's busy right now, on another call but he's going to get back to us."

"They already called a doctor over at PJ's place, a Doctor Flannel. Let me call Lia and see what if he's made a diagnosis yet."

"They're nearly the same," he said.

"What do you mean, nearly?"

He wheeled himself out of the room. No need to worry the Lester's any more than they already were.

He whispered into the phone, "His pupils are still visible, but they are huge. Like sores, about to burst!"

"Oh, gross!" Lia said. "Maybe he should go to the hospital?"

"They've put in a call to their family doctor, but he's unavailable. So, let me know the minute Dr. Flannel gives his opinion and I'll pass it on. You might want to tell him about Arden's eye and see if he'd advise immediate hospitalization."

"Will do. I'll be in touch."

He explained everything to the Lesters. They stared ahead, with blank faces. He was worried about how they were taking it all.

"Would anyone like a cup of tea?" Mrs. Lester inquired.

"No thank you," E-Z said. Mrs. Lester was one of those Moms who believed tea could solve most problems.

Mr. Lester followed his wife into the kitchen.

"Don't you usually join in with their games?" Alfred inquired now that he and E-Z were alone with Arden.

'Sometimes," E-Z said, "But lately if I have any free time, I usually spend it writing. I don't get a lot of time to myself these days."

"Understandable. Sorry if I'm hanging around too much."

"No, it's fine. I have to get more organized. School work is getting more complicated, you know we're on the path to a career and graduation. They want us to know where we're going, and we don't even know where we are yet."

"I remember those days, but you'll figure it out. Anyway, I'm glad you weren't playing the game with them – otherwise you might be in the same state as they are in."

"True. I can't imagine what would frighten them so much…if that's what happened. I mean a game is a game – not reality. It must've been one heck of a competition."

The Lesters returned to their son's room.

"What happened?" Mrs. Lester screeched.

Arden's eyelids were now open, revealing all white interiors. Like PJ, his pupils had disappeared.

E-Z had a feeling of déjà vu as Mr. Lester walked across the room and bent down to unplug it.

"Stop!" E-Z yelled. "Don't touch it!"

Mr. Lester froze in place.

"Mr. Handle nearly got electrocuted when he touched it. Best thing to do is leave it alone."

"Oh, thank goodness you were here and warned me," Mr. Lester said.

"Yes, thank you E-Z. I couldn't manage it if my son and my husband were both hurt. I just couldn't." She crossed the room and thew her arms around her husband.

"Afterwards his computer crashed, the screen cracked, and smoke came out of it," E-Z explained. "So, PJ's computer is sizzled, fried – toast. Whereas Arden's computer is still intact. If we figure out how to get into it – safely – maybe, we can find out what happened to them. First, I need to call Uncle Sam and ask for his help. He's a techy I.T. guy so he'll know what to do."

"Wait," Mrs. Lester said. "Are you telling us that both PJ and Arden are, the same?"

He nodded.

"I always said computers were evil!" she said. "My Arden is an athlete. He should have been out playing sports, not sitting at his computer and wasting his time." She sobbed into her husband's chest and he held her.

"Computers are necessary for school," Mr. Lester. "Our son did nothing wrong and I'm sure he'll be back to his old self any time now. He needs a little shut eye. A little rest, that's all. He'll be fine."

Alfred Hoo-hoo'd.

E-Z received a message on his phone. "Lia says Doctor Flannel told them to leave PJ where he is. He said his eyes should roll back to normal by themselves. He says PJ doesn't appear to be in any pain. His heartbeat and pulse are normal. He needs rest."

"Thank you," Mr. Lester said.

"Thank you for dropping by," Mrs. Lester said. "We will let you know if there are any changes."

E-Z and Alfred left after a lengthy visit and met up with Lia and they all walked home together.

"I can't help wondering," E-Z said, "if this thing with PJ and Arden is meant to be a trial. Eriel hinted that I should be worried about something. That I should even want to pursue it. If it is, I'm not sure how I'm supposed to fix it. Have you got any ideas? Other than getting Uncle Sam to help us to get into Arden's computer – I'm totally at a loss here."

"It's odd, if it is a trial," Alfred said. "Because trials are a thing of the past, aren't they?"

"They are, but if PJ and Arden are hurt, then I'd have no choice but to get involved. Even though the archangels reneged on our deal."

"They both seem so, out of it. What do they expect you to do? It's not like you have healing powers or anything," Alfred said.

"But YOU DO!" Lia said.

"I do, but, when they are usable. I did try, to communicate with their minds. But it was like they were empty. I couldn't reach them. To heal them, there would have to be some kind of a connection. And there was nothing for me to connect with.

"I keep asking myself if I should call for help from Ariel. She is the Angel of Nature. Maybe there is something she can suggest, or something she can do which I can't."

"That's a promising idea," E-Z said.

WHOOPEE

Ariel arrived.

"What's up?" she asked.

Alfred explained the situation.

E-Z asked if this was a trial the archangels were trying to slip in after the fact.

"Either way you have to help your friends," she said. "You want to help them, don't you?"

"Of course, I do, but what I need to do, what action I need to take in a trial is usually more obvious."

"Didn't I hear whispers, about you not being able to take initiative?" Ariel inquired.

"Are you suggesting," E-Z inquired, keeping his voice low so as not to lose his temper. "That the archangels have put my friends into comas to test my initiative?"

Ariel smiled. "No, I'm not suggesting anything of the sort. But, if it were a trial, then what would you do to help them?"

"When a trial is put in front of me my brain kicks into gear. I know what to do to fix it and I go ahead and do it. With this, I have no idea what to do to fix it. They are in medical danger. I'm not a doctor."

Ariel crossed her arms. "What did you try, Alfred?"

"I tried to connect with both of their minds. Usually, if I can heal humans or creatures there is a connection – one which hasn't been broken by an external force. In both of their cases, it was like the door had been slammed shut and I couldn't break through it."

"You've answered your own question then," Ariel said. "Anything else I can help you with?"

"You weren't exactly any help," Lia said.

Alfred apologized.

WHOOPEE

And Ariel was gone.

"You shouldn't speak to her like that," Alfred said. "If she could've helped us, she would've helped."

"I'm sorry but it's frustrating when they don't know any more than we know. They're archangels! They should know something we don't otherwise what's the point in them?" Lia inquired.

"You mean Haniel is always able to solve any problem?"

Lia shrugged. "I haven't had many to discuss."

E-Z said, "Eriel is useless. Any time I've asked him for help he withheld it. Yes, he gave advice. Told me to figure it out myself.

"Like when he summoned me last time, he hinted around some kind of a conspiracy, or connection, he called it.

"When I guessed what it was – playing games – that there was a connection he was still useless. I wish if they would say it. One way or the other, then I can focus on getting my two friends out of this situation."

"See what I mean?" Lia said. "All the archangels are totally useless."

"Haniel helped you, when you hurt your eyes," Alfred reminded her.

Lia turned her back on him.

"Let's hope the doctor was right and they'll both be themselves in the morning," E-Z said. "It's all we can do."

Arriving at home now, they went into the back yard. They said hello to Little Dorrit and watched the sun come up and chatted about their next move.

E-Z went over a few things which had been nagging at him. In The White Room they'd encouraged him to connect the dots. Most recently Eriel helped him to narrow it down.

He went over everything the girl in the store had told him. How she'd taken hostages, like in a game. How she wore a costume, so she looked like an in-game bounty-hunter.

Next, he went over the details of the boy outside of his house. The kid had said outright that he'd been sent to kill E-Z by voices in-game and if he didn't his family would be killed.

Then he thought about Eriel and the other Archangels' involvement in the trials. Now PJ and Arden were involved.

Would the archangels pull them in, to get to him? Was it his fault – for being too slow in solving the puzzle, they'd given him? The archangels said they were finished with him. They'd cancelled the trials and he was glad to see the back of them. Why were they back, trying to make a new connection with him? It couldn't be a coincidence.

He opened his mouth to tell Alfred and Lia what he was thinking about – instead, he landed back in the silo again. Only this time instead of the container being made of metal it was made of glass and he was without his chair.

CHAPTER 6

UPSIDE DOWN

E-Z WAS SUSPENDED UPSIDE down in a glass bubble, viewing the green, green grass of the earth. He was high above it, and his head hurt so much, he feared it would burst and splatter all over the container. But thankfully something was holding him up. What it was, he did not know.

Unlike the other times when he was in the silo, he wasn't secured (or his chair wasn't) fastened into place. The other thing which worried him, hanging upside down like this, is he wouldn't see Eriel coming. Nor would he be able to smell him.

The minute he thought of Eriel, the container shifted. He feared falling. Wanting to grab onto something but there was nothing to grab onto except for the air. He wrapped his arms around himself. Then he felt movement. The glass chamber turned clockwise one hundred and eighty degrees. His head instantly felt better, more clear, and he set his attention on getting himself out. The sooner the better.

Too late though, the thing shifted, then turned another one hundred and eighty degrees. Putting him right back where he started.

"Howdy, Doody," Eriel shrieked as he pressed his face up against the glass. Then he knocked and sang, "Let me in, let me in."

"Get me out of here!" E-Z screamed.

"Calm down," Eriel cooed. "You are here out of the kindness of my heart. I wanted to personally tell you: your friends are in danger."

"You mean PJ and Arden?" Eriel nodded. "Well, I already know that! You great big buffoon!"

"Sticks and stones will break my bones, but names can never hurt me," Eriel sung.

"If you don't get me out of here – right now – then I'll do more to you than sticks and stones can do!"

Eriel tapped his bony finger against his chin. He was after-all still right side up, which was an advantage over the perspective E-Z was in.

"I wanted you to know, that even though your friends are in danger you needn't worry. They aren't in superhero danger." He paused. "A little birdie told me you think we're trying to slip another trial by you...well we're not. Leave them to fate."

"What do you mean they're not in Superhero danger?" E-Z screamed.

Eriel disappeared and the glass container dropped. He flailed, steadied himself. It dropped again. This went on and on, until he was certain his skull would soon be cracked open like an egg onto the pavement.

Then he saw Alfred, over on the edge of the lawn nibbling on grass.

"Hey!" E-Z shouted. "HEY!"

Alfred stopped eating and waddled over. He took in the sight of his friend, hanging upside down inside a glass bubble.

"What are you doing in there?" the trumpeter swan asked.

"Eriel!" E-Z exclaimed.

"Enough said. I'll go and wake Sam. I hope he'll know what to do to get you out of there."

"Good idea and ask him to bring my chair."

While he waited, E-Z cursed himself. He'd missed an opportunity to demand more information from Eriel. He'd acted like a victim. He'd let his two best friends down.

He formulated a plan. When I get out of here, I'm going to find Eriel and I'm going to make him tell me how to save PJ and Arden. I'm going to make him swear he'll never put me in this position ever again.

Wait a minute. If PJ and Arden weren't in superhero danger. What kind of danger were they in? Did they even need rescuing? Or was Doc Flannel right in saying they'd get over it and be back to their old selves soon?

He didn't like the "leave them to fate" statement. He believed that we make our own destinies, and his two friends were in comas. They couldn't help themselves, so he was going to help them. No matter what Eriel said.

Finally, Uncle Sam came out brandishing a large tool in his hand. "It's a glass cutter," he said. "I knew it would come in handy one day when I bought it on one of those infomercials on television. They said it could cut through glass like butter. Let's see if it was false advertising." He cut around the bottom. Slowly. Carefully.

"Hey, hurry up, I'm suffocating in here! If the sun comes up, I'm going to fry."

"Patience, dear boy," Alfred cooed.

"Nearly there," Sam said. He was on his knees, inching forward, as the cutter slit the bottom of the container. Meanwhile the knees of his pjs were sipping from the dewy lawn. "I'm assuming Eriel had something to do with your being in there?"

"Affirmative."

Sam finished cutting, and released his nephew, then helped him into his wheelchair.

"Thanks Uncle Sam."

"You're welcome. Now explain, please?"

"I'm too tired. And I'm too annoyed to explain. Can we please do this in the morning?"

The sun was bleeding red as it pushed its way up the horizon.

In a few hours, E-Z would need to check in on his friends. He hoped they'd be fine. Back to normal. Then he wouldn't have to give it another moment's thought. If not...if they weren't. Well, either way everything would be better after he got some sleep.

"I can explain everything to him," Alfred offered.

"What do you know about it? I had to yell at you, to get your attention."

"Oh, I saw the whole thing. What do you think I was doing out here? I was waiting for you to ask for help. Didn't want to interrupt your Eriel time."

"Interrupt. Very funny. Okay, fill him in. I'm off to catch some zzzs. I'm too tired to think anymore." He wheeled himself up the ramp and into the house and dropped into bed fully clothed.

E-Z dreamed it was his seventh birthday. His parents had rented out the indoor virtual gaming park. He'd invited twelve kids in all, so there were thirteen of them and one team had to have an extra player. As it was his day, they called teams and the last man picked went onto his team. They called themselves the Ball Breakers. The other team, led by Kyle Marshall, called themselves the Bat Shitz.

"You can't use that name," E-Z's team chided. "It's practically a swear word."

"Ah, think again," Marshall said. "The spelling is Shitz. We're named after my dog. She's a Shitz-hu."

"Let's play," E-Z said.

PJ and Arden were on E-Z's team. The tornado trio team kicked the Bat Shitz' team's butts until they were all too tired to move.

"Food is served," E-Z's mother called. The parents were waiting in the adjoining restaurant. They'd ordered a slew of pizzas, buckets of soft drink, and eventually a cake loaded up with candles.

The kids left the gaming area together. Soon Arden realized he'd left his baseball cap behind.

"I can't leave it! I have to go back!"

"We'll come with you," E-Z said. "Give me a second to tell my mom."

"I'll let her know," Kyle who was nearby said.

E-Z, PJ and Arden back tracked. When they couldn't find the cap, they kept on walking.

"It has to be here somewhere!" Arden said.

"I sure didn't think it was this far," E-Z said.

"Those vultures will eat all the pizza before we get back," PJ said.

"Don't worry, Mrs. Dickens will save us some food. She knows we won't be long."

The corridor expanded into another building, another place. In front of them was ginormous guillotine. At the top, above the blade was Arden's cap.

On the blade itself was a sign. It was still dripping red paint, or blood. It said, "Head goes here."

"Are we dreaming?" Arden asked. "Cause, I really don't need my baseball cap that bad."

"Listen. Voices," E-Z said.

Whispers, very quietly, but murmurs. First, it was a lone woman. Then another joined in, for a duet. Then another joined in for a trio. The whispers turned into a chant.

"I can't make out any words," PJ said.

"Shhh," E-Z said, holding his finger to his lips.

As the voices sang,

"B-link and you're dead.

B-link and you're dead.

B-link and you're dead, B-link and you're dead," to the tune of Happy Birthday to you.

"That's creepy!" PJ said.

"Let's head back," Arden said, as the door they'd come in through slammed shut and footsteps echoed along the corridor.

The footsteps grew louder.

CLANK. CLANK. CLANK.

Chainmail. Coming nearer. Booted feet. One soldier. A very tall figure, hooded. Carrying something silver: a knife sharpener.

When he reached the foot of the guillotine, the hooded figure pulled a feather out of his pocket. He put it against the blade. It cut through it like butter. Still, he went ahead and sharpened it further. While he sharpened the blade, he hummed under his breath, like he was enjoying his work.

"As if the guillotine blade isn't sharp enough!" PJ whispered. "Get me out of here!"

Arden ran for the door and started hammering on it. "E-Z you've got to get us out of here! You've got to help us! Please help us!"

MESSAGE LOADING.

PJ and Arden's faces popped onto the screen. They said two words:

"WARN THEM."

E-Z woke to hear Uncle Sam slamming his fists on his bedroom door. "Get up E-Z, we can't find Lia!"

Now that he was awake, he realized she'd been contacting trying to get in contact with him. To update him. He checked his phone. A message with an update.

"It's okay," E-Z said, "she's with PJ. Tell Samantha she's fine. I need to go to see him and Arden soon. Where's Alfred?"

"He's in the garden," Sam said. "Do you want some breakfast before you go?"

"A grilled cheese sandwich would hit the spot. Thanks."

As E-Z dressed he thought about his dream. The guys were talking to him, through a mutual event they shared when they were seven years old. He had to figure out what it was all about. Warn them? Warm who exactly? This was a definite clue but who exactly did they want him to warn?

Yes, he was dead certain they were trying to tell him something, but what exactly? He once again had a sneaky suspicion it all had something to do with Eriel.

First, he went to Arden's house, and the poor guy as before was zombie-like in his bed. A doctor was at his side when E-Z and Alfred went inside.

"What's the diagnosis?" E-Z asked.

"First, get that fowl out of here!" the doctor exclaimed.

Alfred Hoo-hoo'd in protest then waddled away. Outside he munched on some grass and cleaned his feathers.

The doctor looked at Mr. and Mrs. Lester, "How much do you want this kid to know?"

"This is E-Z, he's one of Arden's best friends."

"I know who he is, I've seen him on television rescuing people."

E-Z didn't know what to say so said nothing, but he didn't like this doctor's attitude.

"Arden is in a coma."

"Yeah, I thought so. Oh, so when will he come out of it? Dr. Flannel over at the Handle home – where PJ is in the same state – said he'd be back to normal soon."

"That I don't know. His body is protecting him from something, so he'll wake when he's well enough to do so. In the meantime, I'd suggest someone be with him twenty-four seven." Then to the Lesters, "Might be best if both of you work to hire a nurse. I can recommend someone. If you can work from home, that would be best. I'll check back with you in a couple of days."

"In a couple of days," Mr. Lester repeated.

Mrs. Lester led the doctor out of the house.

E-Z followed. "If I can help, do a shift by his side don't hesitate to ask. I'm going over to PJ's now. Lia is already there, and she texted he's the same."

"Keep us posted and give our love to PJ's family."

"Will do," E-Z said, as he and Alfred were reunited. Both lifted off the ground and flew to PJ's house.

As they flew on side-by-side Alfred said, "I wasn't keen on that doctor. When a person is unkind to animals...I don't trust them."

"I hear you, but he was only doing his job."

"We swans haven't caused any plagues or...never mind. I forgot about the Avian flu – but that happened because of humans."

They landed at PJ's house, where Lia was waiting for them with the door open.

"How are things with you two?" she asked.

"Fine," Alfred said.

"Ah, he's a little miffed as Arden's doctor threw him out of the room, but I'm fine thanks. And you?"

"I'm good, but PJ's parents are losing their minds and there's no sign of recovery."

"Did they call the doctor back?" Alfred asked.

"No. He gave them hope, but nothing else, mostly that he'd snap out of it. But I'm worried he's wrong." She paused, blushing a little.

"Oh, one more thing, when I was holding his hand." She glared at the two of them. "He, well I'm not sure if I imagined it, or if he really did it – but I thought he squeezed it."

"Uh, thanks for staying with him. We should take shifts with his parents, so no one gets too tired. You can go home now and spend some time with your mom. She's probably wondering about you." There was no way he was going to mention the hand holding.

"I'll leave when you do, then," Lia said as they made their way along to PJs room.

Alfred, Lia, and E-Z were now alone with PJ.

"I had a strange dream last night. PJ, Arden, and I were at my seventh birthday – but things did not happen like they did back then. They were trying to communicate with me through an event we shared but I'm not sure what they were trying to say."

"Tell us the dream," Alfred said. "And don't leave anything out."

"Yes, tell us and we'll see if we can help you to interpret it."

"Well, it started normal. Everything was how it went on that day, until Arden forgot his baseball hat and we, the three of us returned to get it."

"So, he didn't lose his baseball cap at the real party?"

"No, he didn't. In fact, he was so obsessed with that cap we often teased him that it was glued to his head. So, this was a significant part of the dream. And there we were walking back to the game area and the hallway seemed to go on a lot long than it had when we left it.

We walked for a long time. Chatting away like we used to do. We didn't realize it at first, we'd been walking for quite some time. Arden considered leaving the cap where it was cause getting there was taking so long, but we decided to get it. He said that the cap had sentimental value to him."

"Interesting," Lia said. "Do you know why he loved the cap so much?"

"He wore it all the time because he liked the team. I never knew there was any sentimental attachment in real life other than to the team itself. And in the dream, at that point, not until he said it. So, then the hallway expanded in size and we found ourselves in a big airy room, like an auditorium. In the centre of the room was a ginormous guillotine."

"What! How strange!" Alfred said.

"It's kind of scary," Lia said.

"There's more. At the top, over the blade was Arden's cap and under it a sign which read: Head goes here."

Lia and Alfred gasped.

"Arden said he wasn't that keen on the hat anymore. And that's when it went dark and we heard heavy footfalls coming toward us. Boots. Clicking in chains or armor. Then the lights came back up as a guy entered with a hood over his head. He went to the guillotine and sharpened his knives, one after the other."

"Then what?" Alfred asked.

"Then a computer screen popped up which said LOADING and a visual of the two of them came on. They said two words:

"WARN THEM."

"Then what?" Alfred asked again.

"Then Uncle Sam woke me up and asked if I knew where Lia was."

"That's not much to go on," Lia said, "Did he love that cap? And who should be warned?"

"Arden's favourite team was and still is the Boston Red Sox. The cap was a gift to him - authentic - he'd never leave it behind, no matter what. Yet, he considered leaving it in the dream at least twice."

"But he wasn't keen enough to stick his head into the guillotine to get it," Alfred said.

"Who would be!" Lia asked.

"I wish we could use Arden's computer. I bet there's a clue on there. I bet he has a file, something hidden I could find. Maybe that's what the dream was about. And why hey gave me the clue."

Lia checked online for the significance of a dream with a guillotine in it in her phone. "It says it represents fear or anxiety. Being singled out or embarrassed about something."

"I think I have an idea," E-Z said as he scrolled through his list of contacts on his phone.

"Wait a minute," Alfred said, "call Sam."

"You're right, maybe I should run this past him first." He speed-dialed Sam, explained the situation. Sam said he was coming right over to Arden's they should meet him there.

"Everything okay in here?" PJ's mom asked. "Would you like a drink or anything?"

"No thank you, but Uncle Sam is going to Arden's and we are going to meet him there. We'll take a look at Arden's computer, find out the last thing he was doing. Pity PJ's computer is defunct."

"That's a clever idea. We heard Arden's parents called in a doctor too, was he any help?"

"No, he wasn't."

"We'll keep you posted if we hear anything," Lia said, as she felt PJ's forehead.

"You're a good girl," PJ's mother said. Then she left the room, fighting back tears.

When they arrived at Arden's house, Sam was waiting outside for them. He had his laptop, and a bag full of computer tools, and some other bits and pieces.

Together they went inside where Sam set his own computer up nearby, a laptop, plugged it in on the other side of the room, then had a look at Arden's setup. It was plugged straight into the wall socket. With no protective power bar for unsuspected surges. Good thing he always carried one in his bag.

After securing the safety power bar, he plugged Arden's computer into it. They waited – and nothing happened. Taking it as a good sign, he clicked the power on, and Arden's computer sprung to life. A password was required. A password which none of them knew.

"Any guesses?" Sam asked.

E-Z typed in Boston Red Sox. He tried Arden's middle name which was Daniel. No good.

"Try guillotine," Alfred suggested.

"Bingo!" E-Z said, now all he had to do was search the history.

"Let me," Sam said, as he clicked into the settings, looking for something unusual. There wasn't anything out of the ordinary.

"What was the last thing he did? Was he playing a game?" E-Z asked.

As Sam clicked to find out, the no surge surge bar caught on fire. Uncle Sam ran to get the fire extinguished, by the time he returned E-Z had already smothered it with a blanket. "Good thinking," he said.

"I hope Arden's mom thinks so!"

"Grab the hard drive!" Sam said, which he did before it was fried. "Now we take this with us, and we see what we can see."

CHAPTER 7

DISCUSSION

AS THEY MADE THEIR way home home, E-Z was still thinking about the "Warn them" message. Could if have been more than a dream?

"I wonder," he said.

"About what?" Sam asked.

E-Z explained about his dream and the message, then added his new idea to see what they thought of it.

"PJ and Arden set things up on the website so we could do Podcasts in the future. I'm wondering if I should use it, once we figure out who to warn. We could sure reach a lot of people."

"That's a brilliant idea!" Sam said, "But shouldn't we be building up a following now? So then when we're ready to convey the warning, we'll already have some subscribers?"

"What would I say?"

"Let's think on it," Lia said. "And we'll be right there by your side."

"I'm fine with doing some of the talking."

Arriving at home now, they went inside.

CHAPTER 8
BRANDY LIVES

WHEN SHE FIRST SAW him, it was music they had in common. She played the piano, better than average but not exceptionally well. Her music teacher said she had a natural ability - whatever that meant. But she could only play songs which meant something to her. Then she'd remember them and be able to play them straight away. However, forcing her to play something she didn't like made her hate taking lessons.

She stuck with it. Forced herself even when she hated it. Hoping she'd be able to fake her way onto the school band.

Her parents wanted something to show for all the lessons they paid for. They insisted she try out for the band – to get more involved with school activities.

"It'll look good on your college application," her father said.

"Try your best, that's all we are asking. Give it your best shot!" her mother said.

However, this year's high school auditions stacked with talented kids. A gifted male drummer was already on the stage performing when she entered the auditorium.

With perspiring palms and a thumping heart, she moved along the line. A line of students and teachers clapped and tapped their toes. She could feel the floor pulsing with every beat.

Like a robot, she continued to walk along the edge of the auditorium, until she was as close to the stage as she could get.

Now she snuck out the door, went backstage. Stood with the other on deck performers and applauded like she'd always been there.

It was a brilliant plan. Everyone had been so involved in his audition, they hadn't even noticed she'd cut into the line.

"Who is he?" she whispered to the girl in front of her in line.

"Shhhhh!" the other waiting performers replied.

He drummed on, decked out in denim, with his blond hair swaying and bouncing. Then he leaned in closer to the microphone and his deep melodic voice joined in with the beat.

She pushed a little closer, and as she did, she noticed an itchiness which hadn't been there before. On her palms, her arms, her legs. She scratched and found no relief. In fact, it got worse and soon it was like her skin was on fire. Then her breathing deteriorated and her heartbeat slowed down.

"Calm yourself," she whispered both aloud and in her head.

It was the last thing she remembered before she woke up in a moving vehicle.

CHAPTER 9

ABOUT BRANDY

THE VEHICLE WAS SPEEDING along the highway. She was in the back seat. Whose car was she in? It wasn't a vehicle she recognized.

She attempted to sit up; her head hurt – like a train was rushing through it. She closed her eyes for a second and listened, trying to figure out how she'd gotten there. The car itself smelled funny, new, and old at the same time.

PFFT.

The vent excreted a smell which made her stomach lurch, and she vomited.

"Hey, watch the interior," a male voice said. "It's leather, the real thing." His phone rang and he spoke into it via a microphone in the visor. "Yes, we'll be there soon," he said. He disconnected then cranked the radio up.

Her hands were tied, not behind her like she'd seen in the movies, but in front of her, just over the fastened seatbelt. "I want to go home!"

"Soon," the male voice replied over the chorus of a Drake tune.

After travelling for what she thought was thirty minutes or so, he pulled into gas station. He locked her in, then slammed the door behind him and left her alone without saying a word.

She looked out the window trying hard not to vomit again. Her captor or kidnapper, whatever he had gone inside. She hoped he wasn't a kidnapper planning to ask for a ransom. Her parents had no money to pay for her return. She focused on the moment, noticing that the doors had no handles and the buttons to open the window didn't work.

On the other side of the car pumping gas, she saw a guy.

"HELP!" she cried, giving it everything she had. Knowing this might be her only opportunity.

When he didn't respond she pounded her tied fits on the closed windows. It was difficult to make any sounds here in this fishbowl of a car. She glanced back and her abductor was returning to the car carrying with him a can of pop and two chocolate bars. When he got behind the wheel, he tossed a chocolate bar over his shoulder at her. She couldn't catch it, she hated that kind, not to mention she'd recently vomited.

"I'm thirsty," she said.

"What do you want?" he asked, then went inside, coming out nearly immediately with a bottle of water.

He unfastened the cap and put it into her hands. Even though they were tied, she was able after a couple of tries to get some water into her mouth. The front of her t-shirt was dripping with water. She didn't mind, it washed away some of the barffy smell.

"Thank you," she said.

Moments later, they were back on the highway again. He sped up, moved into the fast lane and her seatbelt became unfastened. She tumbled about in the back of the car, like a single die rolling without direction.

"Stop that, you lunatic!" the man said, as she attempted to refasten the seatbelt with her hands tied.

The tires as the driver changed lanes recklessly. Other drivers hit the brakes, to keep clear of him.

Then he headed for the off-ramp. He slammed on the brakes, stopped. Got out of the front seat, opened the back door.

She was ready with her feet pointed toward him and struck him with all her might in one major two-footed kick. He fell to the ground and she was out of the car, running wildly when a car hit her, then another, then another.

He got back into the car and sped off.

"Stupid girl!" he exclaimed.

CHAPTER 10

BRANDY REMEMBERS

"**I**T HAPPENED AGAIN, DIDN'T it?" her mother asked, as she helped Brandy out of the grocery cart. "What happened this time?"

"Sorry, Mom," the teenager said, bending down to tie up her shoe. Her hands felt so good, now that they weren't tied anymore.

Her mother bent down and whispered, "Was it the same as the other times? Did you faint?"

She stood up, glanced toward the door.

"Tell me," her mother said, moving her daughter in front of her so they were close and no one else could hear. Besides, no one else was in their aisle.

"I was at school, at the auditions. A boy was playing solo on the drums and singing. He was really excellent."

"And dreamy too I expect?" her mother asked.

She felt her cheeks growing hot. "My heart sped up, raced and my palms became sweaty and I felt funny. Next thing I knew, I was tied up in the back of a moving vehicle!"

"Tied up? In a car? Whose car? Who was driving? Where were you going?"

"I didn't recognize the car, or the driver. He was talking to someone, using one of those hand-free microphones. He was an okay driver until he got onto the highway. Then he drove like a maniac and I pretended the seatbelt had come undone. When he pulled off the road and stopped, I kicked him so hard he fell over and I made a run for it."

"Thank goodness you got away. Did someone stop to help you? I hope you got their number, so I can call and thank them."

Brandy didn't speak, because she was remembering the cars, one, two, three as they hit her, and she died. Again. And wound up at the grocery store with her mother, again.

"Talk to me," Brandy's mother said.

"I died - again," Brandy said "and ended up here. Again."

She sat down on the floor, or rather her knees went weak and she dropped down onto her knees. Her mother followed, like a domino.

They sat together, holding hands without speaking.

CHAPTER 11

BRANDY THEN

"H URRY UP, BRANDY!" IS what her mother had said the last time. The last time her only daughter had died – and resurrected.

When most parents had to go to the grocery store with their kids in tow – they couldn't get out of there quick enough.

Brandy wasn't one of those kids. She preferred stores to parks, sports – most every activity. Taking her shopping was the only way to get her out of the house.

It wasn't entirely Brandy's fault. She'd been born with a rare heart condition. One they said she'd grow out of. So, running and playing with the other kids wasn't an option for her.

Consequently, she'd grown to love the mall, but what she loved most of all was the grocery store. And things were always pretty calm in the food aisles.

Except for one time when they were handing out free DVDs. Brandy became so excited that she couldn't breathe, and they had to rush her to the hospital.

She'd been three years old then.

CHAPTER 12

BRANDY NOW

NOW THAT HER DAUGHTER was fourteen, it seemed to be happening less and less. Still, she wondered what would happen when she was too big to fit in the grocery cart.

"Why here, do you think?" Brandy's mother asked, "Why always you and I only and here?"

"I don't know Mom, but I do know one thing. I want to shop. I want to buy food and drinks and, I'm off. You stay here if you want, I'll be back in a minute. Here, play Solitaire on your phone. It'll calm your nerves and shopping will calm mine."

The woman sat on the floor, as carts came and went focusing all her attention on the game of Solitaire. Her daughter knew her so well. Still, what she was trying not to worry about was how much – no how little - to tell her husband. She hadn't told him last time, when her daughter had died or the time before, or the time before that. She'd only told him they'd gone shopping and it had been stressful.

"I'm ready," Brandy had said, that time when she was a little girl with arms full of cereal and pop tarts.

They headed for the self-serve check-out line then.

"Let me do it, Mom!"

That's what Brandy would always say. She loved watching the check-out person scanned each object. And god help them if the scan was wrong.

Brandy and her mother now finished for the day returned to the car. Brandy sat in the front and buckled herself in. Off they drove, only stopping briefly at the drive-through to get two hot fudge sundaes.

"We got some really excellent bargains today," Brandy said then and she said it again now.

"I know you do love, but I'd still like to hear more about your, uh, incident today. Can you remember anything else about what happened? You must've been terrified, being all alone in a car with a stranger? What I don't get is, how this thing happens. Was this one any different than the other times? You said one minute you were at the school band audition and the next you were in a car?"

"Yes, I was waiting my turn to perform, with the other students. We were all listening to a boy on the drums. He was incredible, singing and playing. I was nearing the front of the line when, ZAP, I was gone."

"Oh, I don't like the sound of that ZAP."

"That's how it happened Mom. First my hands itched, then my legs, my arms."

"You didn't tell me about the itching before?"

"It happens. Usually, I calm myself down. This time nothing worked and, well, you know, the Z word."

"I have to ask, but do you think maybe this happened because you wanted to avoid the audition? I mean auditioning yourself. It's not something you've been keen to do."

Brandy drummed her fingers on the arm of the door. "I wouldn't jump into a car with a stranger to avoid an audition," she said.

"Alright dear," her mother said, tearing up. She'd said the wrong thing – again. She was always saying the wrong things when it came to her daughter's...what should she call it? Her daughter's travelling adventures.

"It's okay, Mom."

They drove along in silence for a while. It was a comfortable silence.

"I want to know how to help you," Brandy's mother said. "For the next time..."

"I know you do Mom, but you're not there when it happens. I have to be able to handle it myself."

"Is there any one thing which always happens – before you disappear?"

"I wish I could remember, Mom, but like last time I don't." She looked out the window, then crossed her arms.

"Well, when we're at home you can practice practice practice. Then you'll be even more prepared for your audition tomorrow."

"It was a one day only audition. So, there's no chance for me this year. Besides, daddy doesn't like it, when I practice, especially when he's working from home. He says it gives him a headache."

"Daddy doesn't mean it like that," she said. "I'll talk to him. After all, you want to play piano, as a job, yes? I mean one day, after you graduate. And I'll call your teacher – ask for an exception to the rule."

"I'd like to hear how that conversation went!" she laughed. "Hello, Mr. Hopper, I'm Brandy's Mom, and my daughter, well, she time travelled into a speeding car with a stranger, then, died. So, could she please audition for you tomorrow?"

"That's cruel," her mother said. "Have you changed your mind, about wanting to pursue a career in music? Surely, they make exception for students all the time?"

"Maybe they do, but I'm not bothered. That I missed it. There's always next ear. Besides, I'd like to be a shopper, I think that's why I always come back to the grocery store, or the clothes store. Remember that one time?"

Her mother nodded.

"After a shopper a piano player, then a teacher," the teenager said, uncrossing her arms and biting her nails.

Her mother glanced at her, "Don't darling. Biting nails is so unhygienic." Brandy sat on her hands. "In that order?" her mother said, laughing.

"Maybe in reverse," Brandy squealed as they pulled into the driveway. "Daddy's not home yet."

She used the automatic garage door opener without answering her daughter. Yes, her husband was late again. He was coming home later and later every night. He said work was keeping him, making him put in extra time without paying overtime. She hated it when he never came home to see Brandy before she went to bed. At least they'd had a snack ready to eat. She'd prepare dinner for, get her settled in her room. That way she and her husband could have dinner together. It would be a lovely night, just the two of them.

"Grab the bags," she said.

"Okay, Mom," Brandy replied as they went inside.

CHAPTER 13

OUTBACK

THE BOY IN THE Outback in the Northern part of Australia, had been living in a box. He was twelve years old when they found him. His body was malformed since he sat with his back arched and his knees up - box-like. Even when they broke it open and let him out.

He couldn't speak, or he wouldn't speak. Until he began to trust again. Then he stretched out and his body relaxed.

He preferred quiet voices, whispering voices. Loud things, loud sounds of any kind frightened him. He'd shake and close in on himself. He'd search for, and cry out for, "Box!"

They'd kept it there, in the corner. Until the people in Sydney said he'd never get better unless it was destroyed.

He helped them do it, with a sledgehammer, nearly as big as him. When it was shattered into tiny bit, his eyes rolled back in his head and he was gone. Away. Somewhere in his mind. Unreachable.

No one knew who he was. Or who he belonged to. What kind of parents, would lock their child in a box, like an animal?

Still, he hadn't been starved. Not for food anyway. And he wasn't dehydrated.

Which meant someone was nearby. They waited, rangers, officers for them to come back – but they didn't. So, they must've known the box in the box was out.

A team of psychologists had cameras set up in the house, so they could watch the boy remotely from Sydney.

Others, from all over the world wanted to "get in on" the observation of the boy. Some were writing dissertations on child abuse, on neglect. They fought their way to the top of the list.

The boy rocked back and forth without saying saying a word. "Box!" had been his only effort. But he knew what was going on. He heard them whispering. Millionaires who wanted to adopt him. He wasn't going anywhere. He was staying put. This was his home.

The boy, who'd never slept in a bed before – or if he did, he didn't remember - did not want to sleep in one now. Instead, he rolled himself up in a ball and slept in the corner on the floor. He had use for the pillow and the blanket they left for him. Those luxuries went untouched.

While they decided what to do with him, a Sister was appointed. In Australia, Sisters are also called Nurses. In some cases, a Sister is also a Sister (a Nun.) Also, a Sister who is a Nurse can be a brother. If said Sister/Nurse was male.

The boy's Sister/Nurse was a kind lady, who always wore her hair up in a bun. She wore a white uniform with matching shoes which squeaked with every step she took.

The first time she tried to throw a blanket over him, he screamed like he'd been attacked by an angry cloud.

"There, there," Sister said. She shivered, then lifted the blanket. She threw it around her shoulders, and the boy gasped.

"It's soft," she said.

She snuggled into it. Smelled it.

"It's very soft and warm," she cooed.

The boy reached out and touched the edge of the blanket. He petted it, like it was still on the sheep where it had originated.

"Would you like it?" Sister asked.

He said no for two days, then allowed her to put it around his shoulders. After that he slept with it, like it was a living thing. Cradling it like a baby, whispering to it. In the end he took comfort in it and would not let the Sister take it or wash it.

On the fourth morning of the boy's freedom, animals began to gather outside on the front lawn of the property. First a female kangaroo arrived. She hopped to the bottom of the porch steps, then sat on her haunches and watched the door. Next, an emu arrived and did the same. Then came a magpie, a cockatoo and a galah. The birds took turns singing and their voices seemed to call the boy out of doors. Before he'd not been inclined to open the door or go out of it. However, when he saw the animals and birds, he went out without hesitation to meet them.

Sister watched him from behind the screen front door. She wasn't fond of dogs or cats or birds – in fact, they frightened her – but these wild animals terrified her. She'd venture out if needed. She hoped they send someone out to help her soon.

The boy stood upon the porch and breathed in the air. He opened his arms wide, wider, then he filled his lungs with outside air. He breathed it in, greedily.

The Sister who wished he was her very own son, watched his chest expanding within his small frame.

Then it happened.

The boy began to rise, like he was a balloon taking flight, only he wasn't a balloon, and he wasn't on a string – he was a young boy.

The Sister ran out. She loved him – and he was getting away. Behind her the screen door crashed.

"WAIT!" she cried, reaching out for him with grasping fingers.

As the boy slipped away. His little feet rising. Taking him out, further. As the three birds carried him, on and on.

She grabbed, but he was too far gone. And so, she watched, as a kangaroo mother raised her eyes.

And the boy dropped down, onto the mother's shoulders. She sat aloft, with his arms around the roo's neck, and off she hopped. Alongside them an emu kept up with the pace.

The Sister, not knowing what else to do – ran inside to get her car keys. She started the engine and followed the boy, until she could see him no more.

The boy who'd once live in a box, had been taken from the human world. He'd gone into the world where animals cared for their own. And this child, was one of their own. He was family.

And the boy sang songs, in the voices he knew from deep inside himself. And he laughed out loud and was happy, as he was carried away, to the place in his heart. The place where he was, what he was always meant to be.

CHAPTER 14

LONELY BOY

IN THE FORBIDDEN FOREST of Japan, a child's cry rang out. Birds gathered, joining in with the song, amplifying the lonely boy's request for help. A Scops owl arrived, frightening the rest of the birds away. She sat, nearby, guarding and waiting.

A car alarm sounded. Its wailing drowned out the cries of the child. He was in an infant seat. One that used to be in the back seat of a car.

"Click, click," and the car alarm stopped, long enough for the driver to hear the faint cries of the child. She and her husband rushed into the forest, where they found the child who was frightened and all alone. Together they comfort him.

Several waxwings remained, watching. Assessing the situation. They rustled their feathers, and twittered. Like they were reporting the rescue of the child live.

The woman unstrapped the child. She held him close and asked him questions he was too young to answer. Questions like, "Where is your Haha, Ko? Where is your Otosan?" (Translated: Where is your mother, child? Where is your father?"

Her husband searched the area. He called out. When no one answered, he looked for signs. Adult footprints. None were found.

"No footsteps," he said, shaking his head in disbelief. To him the forest was not his favourite place. He preferred cities and noise. It was him who'd accidentally set off the car alarm. He'd hope his wife would want to leave. He'd promised her lunch at her favourite restaurant. That's when she'd heard the child and run into the forest.

He had followed his wife, for her safety. In the city, they avoided areas where predators could lurk. Luring unsuspecting, trusting people – like his wife – into danger.

The forest, this particular forest, was alive with sound. Alive, with light. And the child, they couldn't leave the child.

"Let's go," he said. "We'll take him to the hospital, to make sure he's okay and they can check with the police to see who he belongs to."

She held the child close to her chest, running her hand up her back, like a mother would do to her own child. In her mind, he was just that, her child. The child she'd never been able to have, had called for her and she had come into the forbidden forest and she'd claimed him.

"He's mine," she said, first defiantly, then more softly, "I mean, ours. Our baby. The son you've always wanted."

Her husband looked at the boy. He needed them. And he was too small, too young to remember anything before. He already trusted them. No one would know, he thought. And yet, was it right, to take this child, as their own?

"No one would know," his wife said, like she'd been reading his thoughts.

This happened often, after twelve years together. They thought similar things. Spoke at the same time. Finished each other's sentences.

They were a loving and stable couple. Together they had so much to give to a child. Yet, fate hadn't given them one of their own.

She handed the child to her husband and waited.

The birds above could see how her arms trembled. They sang out, encouraging her to take the child. Helping him to decide that the child was now theirs.

She's already claimed him in her heart and in her soul. So had her husband, but he was torn between the selfishness of it. He wanted to do the right thing, not the selfish thing.

"Would you like to come and live with us?" he asked the child.

Although he did not answer, the three of them made their way back to the parking lot. They put the boy in the middle of the back seat, away from the airbags.

The birds and the owl nodded, then flew away into the forest.

CHAPTER 15

A WOMAN

AN OLD WOMAN ROCKS in her chair, back and forth, back, and forth. Her memories are fleeting, like clouds. Often out of reach.

Confusion is moving in. Soon, it will replace everything in her mind with nothingness.

Dementia does not choose its victims according to the sick person's wants or needs. Its purpose - to confuse. To alienate. To erase.

She'd faced up to it, until one day when everything went topsy-turvy.

That's what she called it now, topsy-turvy. Or T/T for short. The other thing had been bad, getting worse. But topsy-turvy meant she wasn't crazy and more than that, it meant she wasn't alone – not anymore.

In her mind, she saw everything. Sometimes it happened in slow motion, like she'd clicked a button on the remote. Sometimes scenes played over and over again, backwards, forwards, on loop. Other times she was in the middle of a goings on, observing firsthand like a reporter.

When it first happened, she was afraid of being hurt or killed. She'd witnessed some hair curling things. But when she realized those around her couldn't see her or hear her, then she was able to relax. Except for the archangels, they knew she was there, but they didn't let her presence be known to others.

Like the time when her mind flew to The Netherlands. She'd settled in, watching the little girl. She'd cried out when the child lost her sight. She felt helpless, as she was unable to do anything but watch. That too, changed, in time.

Then Lia and E-Z became friends, and Alfred the swan was added to the mix. She watched them, listened in. Felt like a unseen unheard member of their team. She watched them work together and grow into firm friends.

Then suddenly, she spoke to Lia in her mind, and the little girl answered. A whole new world opened up for Rosalie.

At first their conversation was somewhat limited. Even though there was a big age difference, the two had some things in common. Like their love for ballet.

Since the archangels changed the rules, Rosalie kept an eye on The Three even more. Still, these exchanges weren't enough to challenger her mind, to keep her mind occupied.

That's when Rosalie discovered The Others. Children, with unique abilities in other parts of the world – and she could speak with them.

First there was Brandy, a teenager who lived in the USA. Then there was communication from Lachie, also known as The Boy in the Box. Third but not last, was Haruto, who lived in Japan. Haruto was the youngest of the lot. All three children had abilities. And she was the lone connector.

For now, Lia kept her connected to Alfred and E-Z, but soon she'd need to tell them all about the others.

Rosalie trembled as the attendants arrived with her food. Red jelly. Her favourite. She ate the first after pouring some cream on it. Cream that should have gone into her coffee.

In her head she said thank you to the girl who delivered the food, because Rosalie couldn't speak. She was unable to speak. Her only way of communicating was in her mind...

Summoning The Three to visit her at the Seniors Residence didn't seem like the right thing to do. For now, she'd let Lia keep her as a secret, and she'd take notes about Brandy, Lachie and Haruto and put them into a book.

She'd have to hide it, from the archangels. She'd keep a secret file. She wasn't going to lose track of these kids, no matter what.

"OH!" she exclaimed, reaching into the top drawer of the night table beside her bed. She remembered a gift. A notebook, On the front it read, "Happy Birthday!"

She scribbled on the first few pages. Not making any real words, then when she got to the thirteenth page. Thirteen for her had always been a lucky number, she began writing about Brandy, Haruto and Lachie. There was so much to write. When her hand hurt, she stopped, flexed it for a while, then went right back to writing.

Rosalie wondered if there were other children besides these three new ones. If she waited a while, they might speak to her too. It would be better to tell her secret, when all the children had revealed themselves.

Rosalie was careful, not to write "Secret" or "Private" on the outside of the book. And she was glad it hadn't come with a key. Those three things would make anyone who saw the notebook want to read it. They'd get curious, like a cat. There were lots of people her age, who were curious. But they wouldn't want to read after they saw the first thirteen messy pages.

She flipped through to the end of the book. Rosalie filled the final thirteen pages with even more messy handwriting. Then put the book and the pens back into the drawer and closed it.

She smiled, leaned back on the pillow, and rested her arm thinking about dinner. Mostly dessert.

CHAPTER 16
WHERE WILL YOU STAND?

THERE IS ONE WORLD in which we live, a world which is filled with both good and bad people. A world controlled by human beings, who are flawed, and imperfect. People who are not robots...Not programmed to be good or bad.

We learn our lives, from what we see, what we notice, what we are taught and what we become.

We learn from the foundations which have been laid out for us. As we grow and expand our horizons, choices must be made.

It's up to us to apply the knowledge learned. To choose between wrong and right.

Through the ages, great people have been fooled. Great and powerful people. Adults even.

Sometimes decision is easy. With no gray areas. Sometimes there are forces out of our control, leading us. Others pushing us to follow their code of ethics. Sometimes there are unexpected elements.

Say we're on a path, and someone puts up a roadblock. We can take it down or stop and wait for the person to remove it. We can choose.

Life is about choices. The choices we make can line us up for life. We follow that road, with the bricks laid out from our good decisions.

Or we can let ourselves be led astray. Fooled. Tricked into going against what we know to be true.

When that happens, everything can tumble down – like dominoes.

And there will be consequences for our actions – or inactions. Not to only ourselves. What we do, affects others.

And in the end, after we die, we're all caught and held in the arms of our Soul Catchers.

The Furies – the three evil goddesses of vengeance – are taking control of the soul catchers.

Soul Catchers are getting highjacked.

Souls are flying around without a home.

Homeless Souls.

Chaos is on the horizon.

Where will you stand?

CHAPTER 17

ROSALIE IN THE WHITE ROOM

ROSALIE OPENED HER EYES. It was mealtime and she'd requested a breakfast tray. Her room was on the way to the dining room. When they carried the food there, she'd smell bacon. It would make her mouth water. And the coffee. She waited her turn. She had no choice but to wait her turn.

She knew that they preferred to feed the residents in the dining room. She understood the need for sticking to a timetable. Still, she knew they'd get around to her – eventually. They always did in the retirement home in which she lived.

She watched a cardinal in a tree outside her window and considered getting out of bed, for a closer look.

But when she threw back the covers, and stepped down onto the carpet – she felt funny. Fuzzy.

And landed in The White Room.

Nothing had changed since E-Z had been there. And it didn't take long for Rosalie to find her feet and start exploring.

As she ran her fingers along the bookshelves, she had a feeling of déjà vu. Had she been to this room before?

She moved to the centre of the room, and turned about. The bookshelves went on and on. As far as the eye could see. The height of them, made her feel dizzy and she longed to sit down and catch her breath.

BINGO

A comfy chair appeared, and she dropped into it. She leaned back, then realizing it had wheels and could spin around, she turned it. And turned it. Then she closed her eyes and rested. Glad she'd not had breakfast yet since her stomach was a bit queasy when above her, something moved.

Or had she imagined it.

"You there!" she shouted, pointing at nothing and no one. "I saw you move, you, you little...whatever you are, come out, come out," she coaxed.

Deciding she'd imagined it; she went back to investigating her surroundings. And wondering how she'd come to be in this place.

"Am I back in my room, imagining myself being in this place?" She used her fingernails to dig into the arms of the chair. She watched as they scraped marks into the leather surface. The marks were light scratches, light enough to be removed with a little a little rubbing. After all she was a guest, and guests should always take care of the place they are visiting. Otherwise, they won't be asked back again.

Above her, something moved again. This time it was accompanied by the sound of wings flapping. Was a bird trapped up there, unable to get out?

"I'm coming, little one," she said, standing up and walking toward the ladder.

The wooden structure, like it could read her mind rolled across the floor and stopped at her feet.

"Hop on!" it said.

Rosalie did, and it wasn't until it moved itself, that she realized the thing had spoken to her.

"Uh, thank you," she said, as it came to a stop.

"You're welcome," the ladder said. "Any book you're after in particular?"

Rosalie laughed. "I thought I heard a bird. Shhhh."

The ladder laughed. "There are no birds in here, Madam. The sound you're hearing comes from the books."

"Books with wings?"

"Yes," the ladder replied. Then, "You there! Come here!"

Rosalie watched as a thick black book pushed itself to the edge of the shelf. Then wings sprouted out of its front and back. If flew down and landed in Rosalie's hands.

"Oh my!" she said, looking at the spine. "Think I've already read this one."

DWOING.

The book tore out of her hands and returned itself to its original position on the shelf.

"I'm sorry," Rosalie said. Then to the ladder, "I hope I didn't offend Mr. Dickens."

"If you're finished with me now," the ladder said, "May I suggest you hop off?"

"I'm sorry to have wasted your time" she said.

"You haven't. I'm pleased to be of service."

Rosalie stepped down and the ladder sped to the other side of the room.

Rosalie felt her forehead, no she wasn't fevered. Her blood sugar level must've fallen too low. And now she wouldn't get to eat, not for hours. And that thief Agnes Lindsay would steal her breakfast. She'd sneak into her room and eat every bit of it. When the attendants returned to pick up the tray, they'll think Rosalie ate it. Rosalie and Agnes were sworn enemies.

To take her mind off her rumbling stomach, Rosalie focused on books. One book in particular. A book she'd loved to read over and over again when she was a little girl. It was called Anne of Green Gables by, by...She could not recall the author's name.

"Lucy Maud Montgomery," the ladder said, as it sped to her side. "Hop one," it said.

"Ah, thank you for the offer but I'm too hungry, and maybe too dizzy to climb onto you."

"Take a seat," the ladder said, "Over there." Then the ladder whistled and high upon the shelves a book moved forward. It sprouted wings upon its front and back, and flew into Rosalie's hands. She hugged it to her chest.

"Thank you," she said.

"Will that be all?" the ladder inquired.

"Yes, unless you have an extra pair of reading glasses hidden somewhere in this room."

BINGO.

Her glasses appeared and sat perfectly straight upon her nose.

The ladder returned to its former position.

Rosalie's ankles hurt.

BINGO.

A stood popped under her feet.

She opened the book. Inside was a sketch of the book's namesake Anne Shirley. She ran her finger along the outlines of the little orphaned girl's red hair.

Anne winked at Rosalie. Who blinked, then smiled in return. She'd heard of interactive books before, but this one took the biscuit!

With trembling hands, she unfolded the map of Canada, Her eyes followed the arrows which led to Prince Edward Island. In her mind she walked the distance – arriving at Green Gables. Outside the house were the Cuthberts. Waiting for Anne.

She turned the page and got to reading. Laughing as she went at every predicament Anne got herself into.

Then Rosalie's stomach rumbled, and she wished for something very unbreakfast-like. A Jell-o Salad.

Something which her mother used to make on special occasions for her when she was a little girl. Her favourite part was the whipped cream on top.

BINGO.

There in front of her was a Jell-o Salad rainbow layered with a dollop of whip cream on the top. She thought spoon and

BINGO.

One appeared. But then she remembered how her mother and father would scold her, if she ate her dessert first. She thought of mashed potatoes. Steamy hot with butter melting on top. Oh, and meatloaf with ketchup. And peas freshly picked from the garden.

BINGO.

In front of her was a huge bowl of mashed potatoes. Butter melted down the sides. It was a work of art. It looked almost too good to eat.

Beside it was a square of meatloaf with a dob of ketchup across the top.

And in a separate bowl, peas. With a sprig of mint on top.

She smiled. As a little girl she didn't like her food items to touch. In this room, the chef knew what she liked.

But the chef had forgotten to give her eating implements. She envisioned a knife and a fork.

BINGO.

Those arrived too. She ate greedily. Careful not damage Anne of Green Gables. The book sensing a need for protection flew up and hovered in the air where Rosalie could easily reach it.

Rosalie ate everything including the Jell-o Salad, which jiggled on the spoon.

When she was finished

BINGO

the dishes, cutlery, etc., disappeared.

After a few moments of thankfulness for the food she'd been given, she looked up at the book.

If flew to her, and she resumed reading.

Reading and waiting.

What, or who she was waiting for – she did not know.

CHAPTER 18

CHARLES DICKENS

IN THE CITY OF London, England, a metal container fell from the sky.

The container itself was not long, or silo-like. In fact, the closest item it resembled was a capsule. The difference was this item was square in shape and had no windows. Instead of windows, it was mirrored on all sides. Also being flat when it hit the water it skidded across with a tremendous force. It landed on the bank of The River Thames.

Watching it all happen, were two detectorists whose names were John and Paul. Both men were in their thirties. They earned a living from the profits of detecting. Therefore, they were considered Professional Detectorists.

The Detectorists' hours varied. They were self-employed and responsible for the upkeep and management of their tools.

A Detector required many tools. He didn't want to be out on a dig unprepared. Most carried a toolbox everywhere with them. Inside were essential items. To name but a few: headphones, rain covers, harnesses, digging tools, trowels, a tool belt, apron (with pockets,) a waterproof pouch, backpack, trash bag.

Most of John and Paul's digs were in London, on The Thames. As required by the law they carried Standard and Mudlark permits. These were granted by Port of London Authority.

The permit allowed them to dig to a depth of 7.5 cm if required (the ladder was necessary whether you intended to dig or not.)

In the case of the square object – which had landed in front of them - some thought needed to be put into it. Before they fetched it and made a claim on it.

"Fancy having a closer look?" Paul asked.

John, who didn't say much nodded.

They trudged forward, tools in hand. Their wellington boots squished and squelched, displacing mud and water with each step. The riverbank was often very mucky, after several days of consistent rain.

"Claim!" Paul said.

"Fair enough," John said.

Although they'd both seen it at the exact same time, he knew that was claiming on his behalf too. They were partners, always had been and nothing would ever change that.

Both trudged on until they reached it. It was like a square mirror ball and when they tried to examine it all their saw was their own reflections in it.

"I need a haircut," John said.

Paul scoffed, as he touched the side of it with the toe of his boot. "There's got to be a way of opening it," he said.

"It's too big for us to roll over," John said, as he took a measuring tape out of his pocket and measured the height of one side. He showed the results to Paul, which read, 60 centimeters.

They walked around the object. Stopping to tap, tap now and then. Careful not to put mucky fingerprints on the mirrored object. But hoping they'd touch a secret button and spring it open.

And listening. To ensure it wasn't ticking.

"Maybe we ought to take it to the museum or report our discovery?" Paul suggested. "They'd send along a truck, or a crane to pick it up and transport it. After the bomb squad at a look at it."

John shook his head.

"If they send the bomb squad over, they'll blow it up. Broken glass will be everywhere, and our claim will be useless."

"True, true," Paul said. "Those guys love to blow things up. I mean, that's a perk, isn't it?"

"I reckon so. What should we do now? It's not ticking. We're clear in that regard."

"Yes. No need for the squad," Paul said. He walked around the object, with his hands behind his back. It was his thinking walk. John followed along behind him, matching his steps, hands behind his back.

Paul said, "We need to figure out what it is and how old it is. We only have to claim certain things according to the Treasure Act of 1996. It doesn't look like gold or silver and it definitely doesn't look over three hundred years old. This find might be ours and ours alone, i.e., we might not need to report it to our local FLO (Finds Liaison Officer.)

"Definitely not gold or silver," John said, knocking on the metal object and listening. It sounded hollow. He tapped it in a few places and listened.

Above them two lights appeared.

One was green and one was yellow.

They landed on the top of the object.

"Shoo!" Paul said.

"Are we going mad?" John asked, scratching his head.

"Don't think so," Paul replied.

The lights lifted off and floated around. Both dropped to the foot of the container. Once they settled, the lights lifted it, and held it in place. Seconds later it began turning, slowly at first, then quickening. Soon it was rotating at a lofty speed. As it spun, it began to sing in a high-pitched voice.

The detectorists fell to their knees and covered their ears with their hands. Their bodies were wracked with nausea, not unlike seasickness. And they were very afraid.

"What's happening?!" John shrieked.

"I think the thing is hatching!" Paul replied.

As the container dropped to the ground, pulsed. Shook. Shuddered. As the mirrored box yawned open, a part of it descending like a drawbridge onto the grassy riverbank.

"Arrrgggggh!" the detectorists cried.

They waited, looking on through the space between their fingers. No longer interested in claiming the thing. No longer interested in its value.

Out stepped a young boy.

"It's a kid," Paul said, standing up.

John also stood and put his hands on his hips.

"Wait," Paul said. "He's dressed like one of those Oliver Twist kids."

"I am re-born," the lad exclaimed, tipping his cap, then returning it to his head. He stretched, yawned, then took in his surroundings. "Look, there! The Parliament Buildings. They've changed since I last saw them. And listen," he said as the clock struck once, twice three times. "Why've they put The Great Bell in a cage?" he asked.

"What do you mean a cage? And it's called Big Ben," Paul said. "And why are you dressed like that? Are you attending a costume party?"

The lad patted down the front of his waistcoat. He checked that his vest was fully buttoned and that his trousers legs were fully down. He was more used to wearing short pants and the longer ones always wanted to bundle up. On his head was a hat which he removed before he spoke again.

"Do you know the way to Portsmouth?" he asked. "Mother and father will worry about me."

The detectorists looked at each other, but neither spoke. For once in their lives, they were speechless.

"I'm off," the lad said, putting his hat back on again.

POP.

POP.

Hadz and Reiki arrived, and blocked flew directly in front of the young boy's eyes.

"Charles Dickens, you need to stay with these two men. They will take you where you need to be. You need to be with E-Z."

"What did they say?" John said, rubbing his ears. "I think I'm going mad."

"They said he's Charles Dickens. Charles Dickens! And we're supposed to help him get to E-Z whoever he is when he's at home," Paul replied.

Charles Dickens. THE Charles Dickens. Otherwise known as E-Z's and Sam's distant relative... Tipped his cap toward the two fairy-like creatures. "I had a book once, with a fairy on the cover by Grimm. Do you know him?" he asked.

Hadz and Reiki giggled, then disappeared.

POP

POP.

Charles Dickens reapplied his hat, "I'm off to Portsmouth." He started walking.

"No, you're not," the detectorists said in unison.

"Course I am," he said.

"Portsmouth is a long walk," John said.

Behind them, the mirrored cube began to shake and rattle. Then it spoke, "This cybus autem speculatam will self-destruct in 5, 4, 3, 2, 1, 0."

The detectorists hit the ground, covering their heads with their hands.

POOF.

And it was gone.

"Whew!" Dickens said. Then he pointed toward The London Eye. "What on earth is that?" he asked.

The detectorists ran in front of Charles. Leading the way and clearing the path. Like two football defenders they kept him safe. Dodging bikes, pedestrians, and stray dogs. Steering him onto other paths to avoid trams, taxies, and scooters.

"It's called The London Eye and you can see for miles and miles up there."

"Any chance we can eat something soon?" Charles asked, rubbing his stomach.

"Why not come to ours and have a cup of tea first," Paul asked. "My mother makes a mean cup of tea and she might even throw in a biscuit or two."

"Sounds good to me," Dickens said. "Then I'll have to make my way home. Mother will be wondering where I am. I'm not supposed to stay out late, and given where the sun is, I expect it'll be going down soon."

When they neared Convent Gardens Dickens noticed a plaque. "Look here," he said. "My name is written here."

John and Paul looked at Charles Dickens.

"What?" he said.

"You will be the most famous British author of all time," John said. "And Oliver Twist is one of your most famous characters."

"Is that so?" Charles asked.

"It is," Paul said. "And I don't meant offend you or anything, but, you know, William Shakespeare is also pretty famous," said Paul.

"Shakespeare was a playwright. Did I write plays?" Charles asked.

"No, you wrote novels. Well then, maybe you were right."

They arrived at Paul's house, "Mum, this is Charles Dickens," he said.

She was in the kitchen, wearing a pinny (apron) and she wiped her hands on the front of it before shaking Charles hand.

"Any relation to THE Charles Dickens?" Paul's Mum asked.

"Lovely to see you again," John said, changing the subject. "Could I be so rude as to ask for a cup of tea with some bread and butter?"

"You three go in and sit down, I'll bring it right in," she said, shooing them out of her kitchen.

They settled in the front room. Paul sat near to the window so he could look out through the net curtains.

Meanwhile John and Paul were thinking along similar lines. How they'd discovered Charles Dickens and how they could make a little cash out of it.

Paul searched, When was Charles Dickens did Charles Dickens die? Answer: 1870. He showed the screen to John.

"Why were you wanting to go to Portsmouth?" John asked.

"I used to live there," Charles said.

"Have you any more books," Paul asked. "I mean books you've not published yet?"

"I don't know," Charles said. "Have I written many books?"

"Yes, you sure have Charles," John said.

"Any good?" Charles inquired.

"I read Oliver Twist when I was a lad and Great Expectations, too. Excellent but a little long for my liking," Paul said.

"A Christmas Carol was a good one," John said, "Not too long and an excellent lesson learned."

The room was quiet for a few minutes.

"I need to find this Ezekiel Dickens – or as he is known to friends E-Z," Charles said. "I don't know how I know this, but I think he lives in America." He yawned ad could hardly keep his eyes open.

Paul's Mum came in, carrying a tray filled with goodies. Everyone ate to their fill, and soon Charles fell asleep in the chair.

"Ah, the wee thing is sound asleep," Paul's Mum said, as she placed a blanket over him.

"He's so little," she said.

"But he's one of the greatest writers,"

John interjected, "Writing is in his blood so he might be one day be a great writer."

Paul's Mum laughed, then went upstairs to her room to watch a little telly.

Meanwhile, Paul and John discussed what they ought to do with Charles Dickens.

"Pity we can't keep him," John said.

"Well, I don't think the museum would accept him," Paul said.

Both agreed to do some research on Charles Dickens on the internet.

POP

POP.

John and Paul stared ahead like they were asleep. Even though they were wide away. Hadz and Reiki sang a song to them which went something like this:

"Charles Dickens is only a boy.

He's not a detectorist's toy.

Help him to find his cousin in the USA.

Do it in the morning or we'll make you pay!"

This song went around and around in John and Pauls' heads until they knew what they had to do.

"We'll find E-Z Dickens," Paul said.

"Yes, it's the right thing to do," John said.

POP

POP.

And they were gone.

CHAPTER 19

ROSALIE BORED

ROSALIE WAS GROWING TIRED of reading Anne of Green Gables. The older she became, the more difficult it was for her to concentrate of any one thing for long. She removed her glasses and wished she had a lavender mask to cover her eyes.

BINGO.

A soft mask with a wafting scent of lavender was blocking out the light and soothing her tired eyes.

"It's like there's a magic genie in here!" she said, then she closed her eyes and drifted off to sleep.

When she awoke sometime later and removed her mask she was back in her bed in the senior's residence. Was she crazy or had she taken a journey in her mind?

Rosalie felt a bit chilly, probably due to the cold sterile environment in which she resided. At certain times in the day, the temperature dropped.

At those times she noticed residents were in their rooms, while attendees tidied up. Since they were working hard, they didn't notice the cold. Not like the seniors did who were doing nothing.

BINGO.

The bottom drawer of her armoire opened, and her soft and fluffy red sweater flew toward her. It steadied itself while she put her arms into it. She snuggled up feeling its warmth as the thing buttoned itself up.

"This is a rather strange event," she said.

She sat quietly, dreaming of a hot cup of tea with plenty of sugar and milk.

BINGO.

A fancy teapot with flowers upon it arrived on a table nearby. When the tea was steeped, it poured itself into a matching teacup, added two lumps of sugar and a splash of milk.

"Three lumps, please," Rosalie asked.

A third lump was added.

The cup of tea on a saucer floated toward her.

"How about a shortbread biscuit or two?" she asked.

It stopped in mid-air.

BINGO.

Now on the saucer were two shortbread biscuits.

"You forgot a teaspoon!"

BINGO.

"Thank you," she said, still wondering if she was hallucinating and/or losing her mind.

Still the tea was hot, not too hot. Sweet, not too sweet. And it went down a treat with the shortbread.

When she'd sipped every last drop from the cup....

BINGO

It disappeared right out of her hand.

She wondered how long these magic tricks, or tricks of her imagination would continue. While they lasted, she'd enjoy them to the full.

"Wait a minute!"

She remembered the book. The one she didn't want anyone to be able to read.

"Can you," she asked the air, "Fix it so the other one who can read my book." She reached into the drawer and held it up. "So, the only one who can read it, besides myself, are Lia, Alfred and E-Z. No one else. If anyone else finds it, and they flip through the pages, they will all be blank."

She waited for a sign. Or a noise but none came.

She returned the book to the drawer, turned over and went back to sleep again.

POP

POP

"Is she sleeping yet?" Hadz asked.

"I think so. She's snoring!"

"Careful not to wake her. But we need to bring her on board – I mean, officially."

"The archangels gave her powers, to watch Lia, E-Z and Alfred. They know about her," Reiki recalled.

"That's true, and she'll loyal to those kids. And the others. The archangels don't know specifics about them – and I think it's better that way."

"Agreed. So, what do we need to do. To make it so?"

"Rosalie," Hadz whispered directly into her left ear. "You want to help Lia, E-Z and Alfred, now don't you?"

"Yes," Rosalie cooed.

Reiki spoke. "And what about the others? Are you willing to protect them? Even from the archangels?"

"Yes," Rosalie replied.

"Very good," Reiki said. "Now, let's give her a memory a boost. We don't want her to forget what she has agreed to do, now, do we?"

Hadz and Reiki sang a song,

"Memories are beautiful things.

Which float around like smoke rings.

Back and forwards, forwards and back

Let Rosalie's memories keep her on track.

Magic, magic in the air and in the sea

Binding our contract with Rosalie."

POP

POP

Hadz and Reiki were gone, while dear old Rosalie snored on.

CHAPTER 20
COUSINS

IN THE MORNING, IN England, while the kettle was boiling John and Paul were getting ready. The computer was on, and the search engine was open.

"I'll make the tea," John said.

"I'll start typing," Paul said, as he keyed Ezekiel Dickens into the search bar. "Oh," he said. "Now that was unexpected."

John arrived carrying a tray of tea, sugar lumps in a bowl, hot buttered toast, with a jar of marmalade on the side.

"Find anything," he asked.

"Have a look at this," Paul said, turning the screen and stirring sugar lumps into his tea.

It was The Three's Superhero website. They watched as E-Z introduced himself, followed by Lia and Alfred.

"Is this legit?" John asked. "They look like three characters from the cartoon network."

Then the recreation of the rollercoaster rescue started. Paul pushed PAUSE. He opened another window. Typed in Amusement Park Rescue E-Z Dickens. A newspaper with an article about it popped up. "It's legit," he said.

"So, Charles' relative is a superhero?"

"Do you think we look at all alike?" Charles asked. He was still half asleep in the oversized pajamas they'd given him to sleep in. He took a slice of toast from the plate, and bit into it.

"You both have the Dickens' noses," John said.

Charles took a closer look at the paused part of the screen.

"Based upon when you were born," Paul said, googling it, in 1812 to now, E-Z would be your seventh or eighth cousin removed."

"What does a cousin being removed mean?"

"It means the number of generations between you," John said.

"So, my ancestor is a Superhero. What's a superhero? Is it like in Sir Gwain and The Green Knight?"

"Ah, I do recall reading that in school when I was a lad, yes, knights and superheroes are similar," Paul said.

John scrolled down to see if E-Z Dickens was mentioned elsewhere. There were YouTube clips of him playing baseball before he was in a wheelchair and after.

"He's quite an athlete," John said. "And he does sport in a wheelchair."

"The game looks similar to Rounders," Charles said.

"Oh wait, here's something about his parents," Paul said.

They read the obituaries for E-Z's parents, about the accident which had taken their lives.

"Poor lad," Charles said. "At least he has his father's brother Sam to look after him now."

"Why don't we just give him a ring?" Paul asked. He flipped open his phone, called information.

Charles looked on over his shoulder, while Paul spoke into it and a woman's voice replied. "I need a cup of tea," he said.

John went into the kitchen to get him one.

Meanwhile, Paul asked for the number of an Ezekiel Dickens in North America. After he dialed and the phone began to ring, Paul put it onto speaker.

"Hello," Sam said.

Charles nearly dropped his cup of tea.

"Uh, hello, my name is Paul and I'm calling from London, England. I'd like to speak with Ezekiel Dickens, please."

"I'm his Uncle, may I ask what this is about?" Sam walked down the hall to E-Z's room.

The Three were watching a movie on the new flat screen television. Sam picked up the remote and hit MUTE. Then put his phone onto speaker.

"To be honest, I'm not really sure," Paul said. "It's not me who wants to speak to him, it's well, it's…"

"Me." A new voice took over the phone. A younger person's voice.

"And who are you?" Sam asked.

"My name is Charles Dickens."

Sam handed the phone to his nephew. "He says his name is Charles Dickens."

"I told you something strange would happen today," Alfred said.

"Me too," Lia said, "But I didn't know it would involve Charles Dickens!"

E-Z hesitated before saying, "This is E-Z Dickens, uh, Mr. uh, Charles. How can I be of assistance?"

Charles laughed. It was a nervous laugh. He didn't know what to say. He'd never spoken to someone who was on the other side of the world before.

"I came back," he blurted. "To find you. John and Paul, my friends, are (he cupped his hand over the phone) – detectorists..."

E-Z hadn't heard the term detectorists before.

"They use apparatuses to find stuff," Alfred said.

Paul took over. "A thing landed in the river. Charles Dickens was in it. Two lights, one green and one yellow told us Charles needed to get in touch with E-Z Dickens."

"What kind of a thing?" E-Z asked. "Was it like a silo?"

"John here," a new voice said. "No, it was a cube. A mirrored cube."

E-Z cupped his hand over his phone, "Doesn't sound like one of those silo things."

"Did the angels send you?" Lia blurted. said "I'm Lia by the way and other voice you heard was Alfred. We're here together with E-Z and Sam."

"Pleased to meet you all," Charles said.

"How old are you?" E-Z asked.

"About ten, I think. Is it true that we're cousins?"

"Yes," E-Z said, "and Uncle Sam is your cousin too."

"We're connected through space and time," Charles said.

"E-Z is a writer, too," Sam said.

E-Z cringed, and his cheeks felt hot.

Sam elbowed his nephew back to reality.

"This is a lot to process, Mr. Dickens, uh, I mean Charles. We'll need to plan to get you here, either that or I can come to you. Can you stay with John and Paul for a bit and we'll be back in touch once we figure out what to do?"

Paul said, "Yes, Mum says Charles is no trouble at all. He can stay with us for as long as he wants to."

"I'll call you back," E-Z said.

The phone disconnected.

"Oh, by the way," Sam said, "There was nothing useful on Arden's hard drive. Other than to confirm they were online together playing a multiplayer shooting game."

"Good to know," E-Z said, that much he'd already figured out for himself.

CHAPTER 21
THE PLAN AND ROSALIE

IN HIS ROOM, E-Z, Lia, and Alfred together with Uncle Sam discussed the conversation they had.

"I can't believe the real Charles Dickens called us on the phone," Sam said.

"Yeah, but what I don't get is why he's here. And what he got here in," E-Z said. "I mean, he's ten years old – he thinks. And his mode of travel sounds weird, a mirrored square box. What the heck is that all about?"

"It doesn't sound like a spaceship," Alfred said, "Not that we know what one would look like."

"Wait a minute!" Lia said.

E-Z looked at her. "Are you thinking what I'm thinking?"

She nodded.

"WHAT?" Alfred inquired.

"Remember when the archangels summoned us, to tell us one of us had to die?" Lia asked.

Alfred and E-Z nodded.

"Think about the container. Like you're back in it again and remember the stuff we found. The papers, we found?"

"I see what you're getting at. You mean the other worldly information. About our lives in alternate dimensions?" E-Z asked.

"Exactly," Lia said.

Alfred bounced up and down on the bed.

"What?" Sam asked.

E-Z explained, as best as he could.

"So, let me see if I've got this right," Sam said. "We all have lives going on, somewhere else besides here. I mean on earth. There are other versions of ourselves, living lives apart from ours. In separate times, different spaces, different dimensions"

"That's right," E-Z said.

"Can we change our lives then?" Sam asked. "I mean, change the outcome? Can we stop terrible things from happening?"

"I don't think so," Lia said. "But I don't know how much they want us to know about the other dimensions. But from what Eriel did tell us, we're the centre. Everything else that happens revolves around us, and the lives we're living now."

"So," Alfred said, "Charles Dickens' being here, has got to have something to do with Eriel and the others."

"Yeah, that's what I'm thinking too," E-Z said. "But why now? The trials are finished. It was their choice. Still, they can't seem to leave me alone."

"Bringing back Charles Dickens. And a ten-year-old version of him at that! It makes zero sense to me," Lia said.

"Maybe when we meet him," Sam said, "everything will make sense."

"Not if it involves Eriel," E-Z said. "Nothing is every straightforward with him."

"It looks like a trip to London, is our only way to find out," Sam said.

"Feels like I wasn't there that long ago."

"Yes, it's easy for you to go. All you have to do is point your chair in the right direction and off you go," Alfred said. "Whereas with me, there is a lot of energy involved with all that flapping, and the wind is a factor."

"You could hop on a plane if Uncle Sam went with you," E-Z suggested. "All you'd have to do is sit in a seat with the other passengers and enjoy the ride."

Alfred hung his head.

"I'm not saying it to make you feel bad. Only reminding you that we're all in the same boat."

"I get that. And thank you."

'Okay, now let's get back to the matter at hand," E-Z added. He clicked the television off.

Lia stared ahead, like she was in a trance. "Rosalie!" she exclaimed.

"Who?" Alfred asked.

Lia continued staring into space.

"Is Lia okay?" Sam asked. "She's barely breathing."

Lia stood. "I have something to tell you. I've met someone, not in person but in my head. She's in my head and I've been talking to her for quite some time. She asked me not to say anything – yet. I think this might be connected with this whole Charles Dickens reincarnation thing."

"We're listening," E-Z said, leaning closer.

"Her name is Rosalie. She lives in a Senior Citizens Home in Boston – and she's quite old. She has dementia."

"Isn't that the one which causes loss of memory?" Alfred asked.

But the minute Rosalie heard Lia mention her name she was transported in her mind and in her body to E-Z's room. She hovered above them, listening carefully to every word being said. She cleared her throat, to see if they could see or hear her – they couldn't. She wished she'd brought along her notebook and pen.

BINGO.

Both arrived in her hands. She smiled and set to taking notes.

"You mean, you two are connecting – through ESP?" Alfred asked. "I thought I was the only one who had ESP?"

"It's not exactly ESP I don't think. Not in the same way you have it."

"How so?" Alfred inquired.

"Rosalie's memories are gone. Most of them anyway. She doesn't even recognize her family when they come to visit her. They don't visit often. She doesn't mind as she doesn't like them. But somehow, we became connected. And she knew all about us and our powers. She's been looking out for us, sort of."

"Why are you telling us this now?" E-Z asked.

"Because she said it was okay. And she also mentioned the White Room. She's been there not once, but twice. The first time, she was returned safely to her bed – but not this time. She says she is there now, and they won't let her go home."

"As you both know, I've been to a White Room," he said. "It's where the Archangels first made promises and told me I'd get to be with my parents again. Basically, where they brought me on board using the trials."

Sam chimed in, "Eriel kidnapped me to the White Room once. It was pleasant enough, at first anyway – until he wouldn't let me leave."

"Yes," E-Z said, "Eriel has tactless. And it is a pretty cool place. You get whatever you ask for by thinking about it – like magic. And there are books – books with wings. But I don't want to go into too much detail here – let's focus on Rosalie. What's happening now?"

Rosalie laughed, thinking what if she told Lia she was in two places at once? No, that might freak them out. She chatted to Lia in her head and told a few white lies along the way.

"She says she is pretending to be asleep. She remembers two dots, one green and one yellow floating in front of her eyes."

"Hadz and Reiki," E-Z said. "Tell her not to be afraid of them. They are the good guys."

Ah, Rosalie sighed. Then she realized this might be the opportunity she's been waiting for. To tell The Three about the others. She thought carefully, then decided it was time to share what she knew.

"Oh wait, she wants me to tell you something." Lia stared ahead as Rosalie's voice flowed from between her lips, "There are others like you, I've seen them. I think that's why I'm here."

"Others, like us?" Lia, Alfred, and E-Z exclaimed.

"I'm not sure how much I should tell them about the other children here in this room. Have you any advice for me? What should I say? Will they hurt me? If I tell them about the other children – will they hurt them?" Rosalie said, through Lia.

"Over to you, E-Z," Lia said as herself.

"Listen to what they have to say first," E-Z said. "They'll tell you what they already know and then you can decide how much, if anything more, they need to know."

"Sound advice," Alfred said. "Always be a good listener. Especially when you're being held against your will in a strange place."

Lia offered, "I'll keep the guys here posted, if you want us to stay on the line – so to speak."

Rosalie spoke using Lia's mouth as her own, "I need to keep all my faculties about me...so I'll say over and out for now. Thanks to you and the gang for help. I'll be in touch if I need you while I'm here. Otherwise, I'll fill you in when I'm back home again which will be soon as I'm missing dinner. Tonight, is turkey, mashed potatoes and peas." She hesitated. "Oh, and by the way Lia, that's a pretty top you're wearing."

BINGO.

"Thank you," Lia said, looking down at her t-shirt wondering how Rosalie knew what she was wearing.

"What?" E-Z asked.

"Oh, nothing," Lia said.

Back in the White Room again. Rosalie thought her notebook would be better served in the drawer of her night table.

BINGO

And they were gone.

BINGO

Dinner arrived. She had everything delicious, but now all she could think about was a strawberry thick shake.

BINGO.

One arrived and alongside of it a slice of Lemon Meringue Pie.

It was then that Eriel and Raphael arrived.

"Oh, oh," the ladder said, as they floated on down toward her looking like they were dressed for Halloween.

"Am I dreaming? Or dead?" Rosalie asked.

"Neither" the archangels replied.

CHAPTER 22

MEET AND GREET

"**Y**OU GO ON AHEAD and finish your meal," Raphael said.

"Yes, we have nothing better to do," Eriel said.

While they watched her eat, Rosalie had trouble chewing. Trouble tasting. And it seemed colder. She glanced at the bookshelves, at the ladder. She had a feeling these two strangers were up to no good as she put down her knife and fork.

"First of all," Eriel began, "this conversation must remain between us and only us."

In her mind, she spoke to Lia. "Are you there, child? Are you listening?"

"...Extinction."

"I'm sorry," Rosalie said, "but could you start again, I mean from the beginning? I'm old and I lost track of what you were telling me."

Eriel huffed. Like a little boy who'd been scolded he opened his wings and flew away. When he neared the top of the library, he crossed his arms and waited. Waited for Raphael to give it a go.

Raphael leaned closer to Rosalie.

"Your glasses are really neat," Rosalie said. "But they are making me feel a little seasick with all that blood pulsing and floating around in there."

Eriel laughed.

Raphael removed her glasses and put them into her black robe pockets.

"My dear, Rosalie," Raphael cooed, "please ignore the rudeness of my learned friend, but we're in a situation here. A situation in which we need not only your help, but the help of E-Z, Lia, Alfred, and the others. You know who I am referring to when I mention the others, yes?"

Rosalie nodded, saying nothing.

"We are a team of archangels and our powers are limited. The thing, which is happening all over the world is happening to souls."

"You mean, when people die?" Rosalie asked.

"Exactly."

"But isn't that more your domain, than ours? You've spoken to God – he knows you, right? And if you're trying to mend a dire situation, why not ask him directly?"

Since Raphael and Eriel did not speak, Rosalie continued.

"From what I understand once a person expires, their body is buried. Or cremated. Their souls – if they exist – live on in another place."

Eriel was in her face in seconds, snarling. "That is incorrect.

Raphael pushed him aside. "It's more complicated than you know. Too complicated for most humans to comprehend."

"Humans are pretty smart," Rosalie said. "We've been to the moon, invented the airplane, the internet, fire. I'm no genius, and yet you brought me here, to convince me."

Eriel laughed again.

This time, Raphael couldn't help herself, and she too laughed.

And laughed. And laughed.

Neither could stop themselves.

Rosalie ignored them. Ignored what was happening around her. The ladder throwing itself back and forth back and forth. The books popping out, then back in again. It was such a racket. So noisy. She longed for the quiet of her room once again.

Anne of Green Gables, she thought.

BINGO.

The book was in her hands. She opened it, found a bookmark, and read. If they needed her help, they'd have to work for it. Now that they'd insulted her and the entire human race, she wasn't going to make it easy for them.

"Good on you," Lia whispered inside Rosalie's mind. "You're in charge. And I'm here with E-Z and Alfred and we've got your back."

Raphael and Eriel were still laughing. Out of control. Bouncing into each other in mid-air, like balloons fastened together.

Then she remembered her Lemon Meringue Pie hadn't been eaten yet. She put the book aside, and pushed her fork into it and took a bite. It was perfect. Not too sweet or too tart, just the way her mother used to make it. She took another forkful.

Above her Eriel and Raphael were in hysterics.

"Stop it!" Rosalie shouted. "You two are the most rude, the most obnoxious things I've ever met. And I've met some pretty obnoxious people in my day." She put down her fork. "Weren't you taught any manners? Any manners are all?" She picked up her fork and pointed it in their direction.

Eriel flew down. He was upon Rosalie, with his mouth open in seconds. She stabbed it into the lemon curd, then forked it into the archangel's mouth.

"Ewwwwww!" he screamed. Spitting it out like she'd given him arsenic.

"Mother always taught me to share," she said with a smirk.

Eriel's pallor changed from black to green. After vomiting he disappeared through the wall.

"I guess he's not a pie fan?" Rosalie said.

Lia was laughing in Rosalie's mind.

Raphael removed her glasses from her robe's pockets, cleaned them and put them back on her face. She sat beside Rosalie. She was so close that she was nearly sitting on her lap.

Poor Rosalie.

"WE KNOW THERE ARE OTHERS AND WE NEED TO KNOW WHO THEY ARE AND WHERE THEY ARE - NOW!"

As she spoke, Raphael's face contorted, into an unrecognizable thing.

Rosalie's hair stood on end. Her body shook.

"Rude people never get what they ask for and you, my dear, are very rude. And so is your friend," Rosalie whispered.

Rosalie returned to the self she'd been before.

Only this time the archangel's tact had changed. And her voice was syrupy when she said,

"I am going to go through that wall and join Eriel. In five minutes, we will return and begin again. We need your help – you're right – and we're not asking for it in the way we ought to." Then to the woman in the wall, "Set the timer for five minutes." Then back to Rosalie, "When the timer sounds, we will return and begin again." As promised, Raphael moved toward the wall and disappeared through it.

The clock in the wall ticked loudly. It seemed out of place. Even too noisy for the library.

"It's very annoying!" the ladder said, moving closer.

"I'm sorry, for all the commotion," Rosalie said. "Me being here has caused you nothing but chaos."

"We like you," the ladder said. "Why don't you move around a bit? It'll make you feel better."

Rosalie stood, expecting to feel tired after eating such a large meal. Instead, she was energized. Especially her legs. They felt like she was ten years old again. She performed a jumping jack. Such fun!

"And now," Rosalie said, "for her next trick. The Great Granny will attempt not one, nor two, but three consecutive cartwheels," – which she did. "Thank you, thank you!" she said, bowing and waving like she'd won a Gold Medal at the Olympics.

BRRRIIIING.

The timer ran out. Eriel and Raphael arrived.

The archangels were dressed differently. Like they were going to two different parties.

Eriel wore a dark pin-striped suit, white shirt and tie.

Raphael wore a red Mumu-like dress which covered her body entirely from neck to toes.

"I feel under-dressed," Rosalie said.

BINGO.

She now wore her poshest frock. It was the one she'd indicated she wanted to wear after she died.

She fell into the chair, with her eyes gazing up. And the archangels floated toward her. Their wings moved, like butterfly wings, as they neared her with grace and beauty. Her eyes welled up.

"How can I help you, dear ones?" Rosalie asked.

It was like they had a power over her now, a power which she did not want to overcome. She fell to the floor, now kneeling in front of the two archangels. Raphael touched her on the right shoulder and Eriel touched her on the left shoulder.

"Tell us what we need to know," they cooed.

"The others are scattered," she said, then she dropped to the floor like a stringless puppet.

"She's too old for this," Eriel said. "If she dies, she'll be of no use to us."

"Keep going, it's working."

POP.

POP.

Hadz and Reiki appeared, each whispered into Rosalie's ears. They helped her to her feet.

"Get out of here you two interlopers!" Eriel shouted with an explosive voice,

Rosalie snapped out of the trance they'd put her in.

"Be gone!" Raphael exclaimed and there was no POP, instead the sound heard was a single

SPLAT.

Rosalie put her hands onto her hips, "I hope you didn't hurt those two darlings. In fact, if you want me to consider helping you, then you ought to bring them back here NOW so that I can see they are all right. I refuse to say anything more to you, until you bring them back." She crossed the room, sat with her back against the white wall and closed her eyes and waited. She had all day, all week, all year. She wasn't in a hurry to be anywhere or to do anything.

POP.

POP.

"Thank you," Hadz and Reiki said, as they sat upon Rosalie's shoulders.

"We are messing this up," Raphael said. Then to Hadz and Reiki, "You know the situation the earth is in, can you help us to attain the help of this human?"

Reiki said, "We know there is a situation! Ff you hadn't reneged on the deal with E-Z, Lia and Alfred, they'd already been on board. Rosalie doesn't trust either of you."

Hadz said, "And you haven't been honest with her."

Reili said, "With humans trust and honesty are everything."

Eriel surged toward them.

Raphael held him back before she said, "An error has been made, on our part and this error has cause and effect. We are trying to save the earth from collateral damage. The only way we can do it, is to call upon those who have been given powers, supernatural, superhero powers. Without them, humanity will fail – and it will be our fault."

Rosalie stood up. She glanced at the two little creatures who were sitting on each of her shoulders. "Can I trust these two?"

"Raphael is trustworthy," Hadz said.

"But we're not sure about him," Reiki said.

POP.

POP.

Both disappeared, in fear of being sent back to the mines by Eriel.

Eriel rose, higher and higher, then disappeared through the ceiling.

Rosalie changed the subject. "While I have a think about it, can you explain what this place is? I call it The White Room, but is that the correct name – and why is it that whenever I wish for something, it appears? Perhaps it is named the Magical Room?" At that moment, Rosalie thought about E-Z, the angel/boy in the wheelchair.

ACK.

E-Z arrived.

"Whoa!" he said, realizing he'd joined Rosalie in the White Room. He thought about his sunglasses and

PRESTO

They were on his face. He walked around the room, getting the feel of his legs and the floor once again. Then he extended his hand and said, "You must be Rosalie."

'And you must be E-Z, she said, "Without your wheelchair. This place really is magical!"

"And, hello, Raphael."

"Welcome, E-Z," Raphael said. Then to Rosalie, "So much for discretion – this was meant to be confidential."

"Whatever promises she's making to you, she'll break them. She's useless at keeping her word – and Eriel is even worse as is Ophaniel – and you haven't even met her yet. Still, letting you know that they're all a bunch of liars."

"I figured that out," Rosalie admitted. "And he left, Eriel acts like a spoiled child."

"I would have liked to have seen that" E-Z said. "It sounds very un-Eriel-like, but man, it would have been an awesome thing to see."

"Enough of these cordialities," Raphael said. "I have no choice I guess, but to explain the situation to you also." She stomped her feet and her wings dropped to her sides in a sulk. She turned to face E-Z and Rosalie. "The world needs saving, due to an error on our part. Do you and the others want to help us to rectify the situation – I mean to save the earth, or not?"

Rosalie and E-Z exchanged glances.

"You go ahead," she said. "I'm on board with whatever you decide."

E-Z did not answer immediately.

"If you tell me everything, I'll convey it to the others, and we'll take a vote. We're a democratic group."

"How long with THAT take?" Raphael scoffed. "And how will you get back to me? Shall I perhaps, keep Rosalie here as a prisoner until you figure it out? Will twenty-four-hours be enough time?"

Rosalie said, "I don't mind staying in this room. There are plenty of books to read and I can order anything I want. Much more interesting and exciting than being in the home."

E-Z nodded. To Rosalie he said, "Thank you and you're right this room is pretty special. You'll be safe here." Then to Raphael, "Rosalie will not be your prisoner, in fact she will be your guest." A book flew off the shelf and landed in his hand. It was Harry Potter and the Chamber of Secrets.

"I'd like to read that," Rosalie said. The book left E-Z's hand and flew toward Rosalie. She caught it and opened it and immediately began reading.

"Rosalie will be our guest," Raphael said. "Twenty-four-hours then?"

"Twenty-four hours," E-Z agreed.

"Wait!" a voice screamed. A voice without a body. A voice which echoed and echoed. Until a book became dislodged from a shelf above. It plummeted toward the floor, until its wings burst forward and saved it from breaking its back.

Raphael looked startled by the voice. She tried to retreat, but something held her back.

Rosalie and E-Z waited and listened.

"Raphael hasn't told you everything," the thundering voice said.

It was like the air was vibrating with every syllable, but in a good, kind, and gentle way, not in a scary end of the world way.

"Tell us," E-Z said.

"A little more quietly," Rosalie suggested. "I'm old, but not deaf you know!"

"Sorry," the voice said. He cleared his throat. Then whispered, "E-Z Dickens, do you remember the choices we gave you? The two choices?"

E-Z remembered them well enough. One was to remain in the silo forever. The memories of his family on loop. The other was to return to his life with Uncle Sam.

"Yes."

"Tell me what you remember about the choices?" the voice asked.

"They said I could remain in the container and relive memories of my family on loop or return to my life with Uncle Sam."

"And the soul catcher? What of it?"

"Nothing," E-Z admitted with a shrug.

The voice bellowed – like speaking now was causing it pain. The shelves shook and things POPPED in and out in mid-air randomly. First there was a giant pickle.

The green object spun clockwise, then anticlockwise, then disappeared.

Next a mirror ball appeared above them. It changed colours as it spun. When it was turning far too quickly, they feared it would crash down on them. They moved take cover but before they made it, the ball disappeared.

Next, the head of a clown appeared. It floated in front of them, and said, "What's black and white and black and white, and black and white and black and white."

"Enough!" the voice thundered.

"I'm sorry," Raphael said.

"You should be!" the first voice quaked. Then quieter, more gently, softly he said, "E-Z and his team need to know about Soul Catchers – everything. Otherwise, they won't understand the complexity of the breach."

The voice paused for a few seconds, then continued, "A Soul Catcher catches souls when a human body dies. It's a never-ending resting place. All humans and all creatures have vessels to go to. The thing you called a silo is a soul catcher. A resting place for all eternity."

"Okay," E-Z said. "So, what's this got to do with the end of the world?"

"I want to see my Soul Catcher," Rosalie said.

"If you and your friends don't DO SOMETHING, no one will have a Soul Catcher. When your body dies, you'll DIE. That's it. End of. Your soul and everyone else's souls will have nowhere to go and when a soul has nowhere to go, then there is no purpose. No reason for it to exist anymore. And without souls, humans are mere meat suits."

"Wait a minute," E-Z said. "Are you saying that the person who is responsible for the Soul Catchers. Whatever you call them – CEO, President, you get the gist. Are you saying they've been compromised?"

Raphael opened her mouth to answer but E-Z wasn't finished speaking yet.

"How does this whole Soul Catcher thing work anyway? I've been summoned to mine on several occasions, and I'm not even DEAD. Are you saying these whatever they are, can now force me into my Soul Catcher at whim?" He hesitated, "And what do you know about Charles Dickens? He arrived in a mirrored container, so not a Soul Catcher. How did his soul get from one place to another? Is his resurrection down to you archangels?"

Raphael waited to see if he had more questions.

He did.

"And what about my two best friends PJ and Arden. How do they fit in? They're both in comas. I want to bring them back. Will helping you, help them?"

The voice in the wall thundered in response.

"No one runs Soul Catchers. It's not like a company set up for profit. When someone dies, their soul is caught, and it lives in the assigned Soul Catcher."

"I don't get it," E-Z said. Then, "Wait a minute, has someone or something hi-jacked the Soul Catchers? And if the answer is yes, then I will definitely need more information on who they are before we get involved. If you archangels can't beat them, then how do you expect us to?"

The voice in the wall said to Raphael, "Well, Eriel was wrong when he said this boy is as thick as a brick. He's got it, in one go. Well done, E-Z."

"Uh, thanks, I think," he said. "But what exactly did I get right?"

The voice continued. "Three goddesses have indeed highjacked the soul catchers."

E-Z opened his mouth to speak, but before he could the voice spoke again.

"Charles Dickens did not arrive in a soul catcher, as you suspected. Blood relatives have powers over time and space. You summoned him. He came to help you."

"I didn't summon him!" E-Z said.

"And yet, he's back and he knew your name and wanted to help you, is that right?"

E-Z nodded.

"And to your last question, yes, your friends' lives are in jeopardy because of the three goddesses."

"Goddesses?" E-Z repeated. "Like in Greek mythology? Are they real? I thought all those stories were fiction."

"They are based upon historical facts," Raphael said.

"We can't go up against a team of mythological goddesses!" E-Z exclaimed. "We're kids."

"The risks are far greater if you don't as we have no one else to ask to help us. There's no Batman, no Spiderman, no real-life Superheroes. The only heroes are you kids, can you? Will you help? We know how, to solve this problem, we need bodies, people on the ground. Humans with powers can win. You can beat this, thing. These things. For one thing, you can SEE THEM. We can't," Raphael said.

"I know you need help, but I can't see how we can save the day – not against powerful goddesses. Yes, we have powers, but what exactly are we up against? What will be expected of us? What are the dangers to us? I mean, you are already dead – we're not. If we help – what are the risks?"

He hesitated, and when no one said anything he continued.

"If we agree, can you protect my Uncle Sam, his wife Samantha and the babies? Can you ensure PJ and Arden won't land up dead in Soul Catchers? And what's in it, for us? After all we'd be risking our lives. You're not human so you 've got nothing to lose!"

Rosalie interjected, "E-Z I don't see as you have a choice. You're right, there will be risks and I'm not dead yet – but I'm old – so the risk to me isn't so great. Besides, I like the idea that when my life ends, there will be a soul catcher waiting for me."

E-Z nodded. "I get that. The idea that my parents are floating around. Alone. Homeless. Soul catcher-less. Well, it makes me sick. It makes me so mad I want to spit. But I still need to talk to the others," E-Z reiterated, crossing his legs. It felt so good to be able to do simple things like crossing his legs.

You're turning into quite the speechmaker there Lia said to him in his head.

"Uh, thanks," he replied.

"As you were then," the voice said. "Twenty-four hours. In the meantime, Rosalie will remain here with us."

"As your guest," E-Z stressed.

"I'll be fine," Rosalie said. "And I'll keep in touch by chatting to Lia. Lia and I love to chat."

He nodded. With Lia, via Lia. E-Z wasn't sure what they knew and what they didn't – but he wasn't going to give them anything they already didn't have.

"See you soon," he said, waving good-bye.

Then he was back in his wheelchair again. He was face to face with his friends. But how could he tell them? How could he explain?

In the end he decided the best action was to blurt it all out. Which is exactly what he did.

CHAPTER 23
CH-CH-CH-CHANGES

ALTHOUGH E-Z'S NEWS WAS not what they expected to hear, both Alfred and Lia had plenty to say in response.

"They have some nerve!" Alfred exclaimed. "After what they did to us. I mean making promises then reneging and changing the game plan. I for one, don't trust any of them as far as I can throw them."

"This is huge, and it involves our loved ones who've died," E-Z said.

"How so?" Sam asked.

"I don't know the specifics. All I know is it involves three evil goddesses whose plan is to highjack and control all the Soul catchers."

"That's crazy!" Lia said. "Why would they want them? Why go to all that trouble? What's in it for them?"

"Hold on," E-Z said. "I'll tell you everything they told me. Keep in mind, they don't know for certain either.

"Anyway, here goes. They are mythological goddesses, who've been brought back. Their goal is to control the Soul Catchers - by any means possible.

"And the way they've chosen to do it, is to kill people. People who weren't meant to die! And then they put them into Soul Catchers they've hijacked. From people who need them. So, their souls have nowhere to go."

"I still don't get it," Lia said.

"Think of it this way. Lia, you, Alfred, and I have been in our Soul Catchers already. Few are allowed in there before they're dead. I mean who would want to be?"

"Agreed," Alfred said.

"Ditto," Lia said.

"But what if I told you right now, that your Soul Catcher has been filled by someone else – and so it's no longer yours?"

"Humans don't even know about Soul Catchers!" Alfred exclaimed. "Most think their souls are going to heaven (or if they are bad to the hot place.) If they knew, they'd be upset about it. But they don't."

"Yes, you can't miss something you know nothing about," Sam said. "Nor can you fight for something you don't know about."

"They told me my parents' souls could be floating around right now, homeless. That hit me hard."

"Which is exactly why they told you!" Sam said. "It's outright manipulation."

"No, it's emotional blackmail," Alfred said. "But I get why they said that. If they told me the same about my family, I'd want to get involved. I want to fight these goddesses. If I was a hothead, I'd act immediately based upon my emotions. But we need to be logical here. We have to keep level heads."

"Who are these goddesses anyway? What do we know about them?" Lia asked.

"And are we certain the archangels are on the right side of this?" Sam inquired.

"They said an error on their part, caused this even to occur – but they didn't tell me exactly how it happened or why. And they weren't in the mood to be pressed for information – anymore than I was already able to get out them. Besides, they have Rosalie and our time for making a decision is running out."

"Exactly," Lia said. "And yet, how can we decide when we don't even know what we're up against? They know we're kids. Yes, we each have unique powers – but are they enough? If the archangels can't manage this situation themselves...why do they know that we'll be able to?"

"That I can't say. I did press them to tell me more. If it weren't for the voice in the wall – they wouldn't have told me as much as I did learn."

"How dare they hold back information from us!" Alfred exclaimed.

"I've explained what I know. There are three of them. They are goddesses – mythological creatures which I thought weren't real."

"We can find out everything we need to know to arm ourselves against them online," Sam said. "But it will take some time." He hesitated. "However, I don't think we'll have much luck searching for information on Soul Catchers."

"I already tried and couldn't find anything."

"When did you first hear about them?" Sam inquired.

"The voice in the wall implied I'd been told about them before, but every time I try to remember it's like a wall is blocking the information."

"Whoa! The exact same thing happens to me," Lia said. "That is so weird."

E-Z glanced at the time on his phone. "Well, I've given you all lots to think about. We have until the morning to make a firm decision...but I don't think we have any choice other than to agree to help them. I mean if we don't then who?"

"I was thinking the same thing," Alfred said. "But I still don't like the way they've gone about it."

"Me either," Lia said. "I'm off to bed. Night everyone. See you in the morning." She closed the door behind her.

"Anything you need?" Sam asked.

"No, I'm good. Night Uncle Sam."

"Night E-Z. Have to tell you how proud I am of you and how proud your parents would be."

"Thanks."

"And good night Alfred," Sam said as he opened the door.

"Good night," Alfred said, then he settled in with his head under his wing and drifted off to sleep.

E-Z, unable to sleep, stared at the ceiling with his hands behind his head. He did a few sit-ups, then turned onto his side hoping to nod off. Instead, he spotted two lights, one green and one yellow floating toward him.

"Are you awake?" Hadz asked.

"No," E-Z said with a smirk as he sat up.

"We're not supposed to talk to you," Reiki said, "but we have to talk to you, so you need to guess what we're not supposed to tell you."

"Guess? Seriously? Can you give me a hint...you know, narrow down the field for me, even a little?"

The wanna be angels whispered to each other. They seemed to disagree, as Hadz flew to the one side of the room and Reiki to the other.

"K, I'm off to sleep. When you figure it out, you can tell me in the morning."

He nodded off, then woke up. He was in his chair and soaring across the sky. He fastened his seatbelt. "What the?"

"We decided as we couldn't narrow the field down for you. Or tell you what you need to know. To make an informed decision... That we'd SHOW YOU instead. So, follow us."

As the clouds zipped by and the clean but cool night air filled his lungs, E-Z felt more alive than he'd felt in a while. In some ways he missed being summoned for the trials to help and save people who were in trouble.

Ever since he stopped working with the Eriel, he hadn't felt like much of a superhero. True, he'd saved a cat who was stuck up a tree. And he'd prevented a baseball from smashing a valuable stained-glass church window.

But most of his day-to-day life was thinking about the future. Planning to finish high school in the best position to attain a scholarship. To the best college or university, he could get.

Uncle Sam and Samantha were planning for the new baby. They were keeping whether the baby was a boy or girl a secret, and no one was allowed into the baby's new room. E-Z thought it was weird to be fifteen years old and going to be an Uncle soon, but he was looking forward to it.

And Lia, she was doing well at school, fitting in even though she'd gone from age seven to twelve in two jumps in a relatively brief period of time. Whatever was aging her seemed to have stopped and now it seemed she had a crush on PJ. She was definitely growing up and he smiled thinking about how bossy she'd become. That reminded him of Little Dorrit the Unicorn. They hadn't seen her since the trials. Maybe the archangels had sent her to help Lia when they were all connected. Then there was the arrival of his cousin Charles Dickens. And PJ and Arden were stuck in comas – and no one knew how to get them out of it. Alfred kept himself busy, around the house. Since he arrived Uncle Sam didn't need to cut the grass as often.

He recalled the two trials again he'd found similarities in. The one with the girl dressed up as a a multi-game player character. The other with the boy who'd been told to kill E-Z to save his family's lives. They were connected. Eriel was right. He just had to figure out exactly what it meant.

"Are we nearly there yet?" he asked, noticing how cold it was getting. They were moving fast, getting closer to Death Valley National Park, in the Mojave Desert. It was December, one of the coldest months of the year for the desert at night and he wished he'd brought his hoodie. It was so dark that the stars looked a million times brighter. Like eyes in the sky with barely a finger's gap between them or so it seemed.

The angels in training didn't answer. They descended a few feet, then continued flying ahead at full speed.

"Great!" he said. "Let me know when we're going to land. I sure do wish I had a travel agent to tell me what it is I'm seeing."

"Use your phone," Lia and Alfred whispered. Then they were silent.

On they flew, over Badwater Basin, the lowest point in North America. It was so named, as the water is bad – therefore undrinkable because of excess salts. But some wildlife and plant life can flourish in the area such as pickleweed, insects and snails.

Deeper they went into Death Valley, while E-Z took in the terrain and tried not to think about how thirsty he was.

"Are we there yet?" he asked again as a black bird flew over his head dropping a load of poop before it continued on its way. "Welcome to Death Valley," he said, wiping it off with the back of his sleeve. He hurried on to catch up with Hadz and Reiki.

CHAPTER 24

DEATH VALLEY

"**H**urry up!" Hadz and Reiki said. "We're nearly to Rhyolite."

He pushed ahead, catching up with them. "And what exactly is in Rhyolite?"

"A little background," Hadz said. "Unless you've heard of it already?"

E-Z shook his head. He'd learned about The Grand Canyon in school, mostly about how it was formed.

Hadz continued, "Rhyolite was once a flourishing town during the Gold Rush in 1904. It didn't last long though, in 1924 it's last resident died, and it turned into a ghost town."

"What does the word Rhyolite mean?"

Reiki answered, "It's an acidic volcanic rock – the lava form of granite. It was named by a geologist named Ferdinand von Richthofen in 1860. Its origins are Greek, from the word rhyax which means a stream of lava."

"So, the town had a big gold rush and they named it after a volcanic rock?" He hesitated. "Think I remember something from class about volcanic action."

"That's correct," Hadz said. "Dating back to two million years ago."

"So, this lesson is interesting and all – but I'm still clueless as to why we're heading to Rhyolite."

Reiki blurted, "Because it's the headquarters for the renegades."

"The ones who are vying for control of the Soul Catchers."

"Who are they exactly, and how can we stop them? By we - I mean us, The Three. Because Eriel and Raphael are holding Rosalie and by the way, time is running out. They only gave us twenty-four-hours to get back to them."

"Shhh," Hadz said. "They have extraordinary hearing, and the wind may carry our voices back to them in whispers. From this point on we'll speak only with our minds."

E-Z asked, using his mind, "What happens if they know we're here? I mean, won't they be able to see us?"

"Hadz and I aren't human, so we're off their radar. You, however, are not which is why we've shielded you."

"Great! There's an invisible protective shield around me – that's handy information for me to know."

In the distance he could see the Black Mountains. "I bet when the sun bakes the heat into those mountains you could fry an egg on them." He hesitated, "What about that bird that pooped on me? Could the baddies have sent it out, to look for us?"

Hadz and Reiki shook their heads. "We saw the bird. It was a raven – known to as a carrier of messages from the heavens."

"Okay, fair enough. I didn't think it looked like a raven. Tell me what it is that has highjacked the soul catchers and what we are going to have to do to beat them." He hesitated, "And what this has to do with the reincarnation as a young boy, of Charles Dickens." He hesitated again. "Also, will Lia get transport? Will the unicorn Little Dorrit return if/when we agree to help you?" That was a lot of talking. He was thirsty and wished he'd brought a bottle of water.

POP.

One appeared. He drank it back after saying "Thanks," to no one.

Reiki asked, "Have you ever heard of Erinyes?"

E-Z shook his head.

"Also known as The Furies," Hadz said.

"I have no idea what either are...but I have a vague memory of something from a game maybe?"

"They are known collectively as the Goddesses of Vengeance."

"Tell me more. Who are they taking vengeance on?"

"Why, the entire human race!" Hadz huffed.

"My friends and I talked about this earlier. Most humans don't know about Soul Catchers. Most believe we have souls. Souls which go to either heaven or hell – depending on the choices we make in our lives."

"Yes, we are aware of this," Hadz said.

"Then tell me," E-Z asked. "Where is god in al l this? God or Jesus, Allah, Buddha...whatever you know him as. Where is he?"

Hadz and Reiki stared ahead without answering.

"Okay, I get it you can't answer that question. Answer me this one instead. Why are the goddesses punishing humans using something they aren't even aware of? I get that they are evil, but it sounds ridiculous nevertheless."

"The children," Hadz said.

"They punish the unpunished. But..."

"Ah, I was waiting for a but... Go on."

"The Furies – Goddesses of Vengeance are abusing their powers. Pushing the boundaries. They are targeting innocents. Innocent children who are playing a game."

"Wait, do you mean, kids playing games are being punished for things they do within the game? But game play isn't real! How can they be punished in real life for something which isn't real?"

"I know that, and you know that, but, to The Furies – Goddesses of Vengeance it's all the same. If in a game to kill someone, you go through the same thought process a murderer would. It involves planning it out, with intentions to kill and then going through with it. In some cases, mass murders are involved. And yes, it is innocent, and they are being asked to do those things in order to get further in the game. To The Furies, the children are the unpunished and they are fair game when they are within the game."

"Wait a minute!" E-Z exclaimed. "What exactly are you saying here? I think I'm getting the gist, how the Soul Catchers fit in, but the idea is so evil...I don't even want to think it, let alone to say it."

"The Furies – Goddesses of Vengeance are taking vengeance upon game players. Those who have sinned in their hearts," Reiki said. "They aren't meant to die! Their Soul Catchers aren't ready to accept their souls and so..."

"They have nowhere to go," Hadz said.

"And The Furies – Goddesses of Vengeance are amassing them here, by creating their own tribe of Souls. They store the souls of the children in stolen Soul Catchers."

"This is creating chaos," Hadz said.

"So, you kids have got to help."

"Wait a minute!" E-Z said. "Wait a doggone minute!"

CHAPTER 25

FOUR EYES

"OH, OH," HADZ YELLED, as a dark cloud was moving quickly across the sky and heading in their direction.

"They can't have penetrated the protective shield!" Reiki exclaimed.

E-Z glanced over his shoulder. What he saw was a black something which was not a cloud. For it was snakelike. With a forked tongue licking the air. Instead of two eyes, it had numerous eyes. Too numerous to count. Each with blood dripping down. Blood and steaming yellow pus.

The tongue of the thing shifted from right to left. Making a whipping sound, while its jaws snapped open and closed. And from its throat a gnarling sound, which alternated between a screech and a buzz.

With the wind behind it, a stench most foul filled the air and soon reached E-Z, Hadz and Reiki's nostrils.

The smell was most foul. Worse than sulfur. Or rotten eggs. More disgusting than septic fluid and rotting corpses combined.

The trio moved up higher, so they could see past a ridge they hadn't noticed before. Behind it, were silver containers. Soul Catchers. As far as the eye could see.

"So many! Are all those filled with children? Oh, no!" E-Z said with a nasal tone since he was still plugging his nose. Although he could still smell the stench.

PTOOEY.

They dodged a spray of ooey gooey yellow pus.

"What the heck is that?" E-Z exclaimed.

Below was a giant eyeball could be seen. It had been closed. Disguised.

PTOOEY. PTOOEY. PTOOEY.

"Oh no!" E-Z exclaimed. "Eye boogers!"

It shot at them, firing its hot, sticky liquid.

"Hold on!" Hadz and Reiki shouted.

Each grabbed hold of one of E-Z's ears.

"Ahhhhh!" he cried.

PTOOEY.

E-Z dodged that booger, but it nearly connected with his wheelchair.

FIZZLE.

POP.

POP.

E-Z was back in his bed again. Beads of perspiration dripped down his forehead.

Meanwhile Alfred continued to snore away at the end of the bed.

"That was a little too close for comfort!" E-Z said. "Did they penetrate the protective shield? Did they see us? Do they know who I am, where I live?"

"No, we got out of there before they could get through," Reiki said.

"Maybe this is a dumb question, but why didn't you just POP us in and out of there in the first place. Instead of taking the time to fly all the way there – and putting our lives in danger?"

"We had to SHOW you."

"Before the battle... What do you they call it..."

"You mean reconnoiter?" E-Z asked.

"Yes, that's right. We had to show you. You had to see it, with your own eyes. All of it. What you're up against," Hadz said.

"We figured what you'd learn, would be worth the risk."

"I guess time will tell," E-Z said.

"Sorry, if we went too far," Hadz said.

"We really did have your best interest at heart."

"I know you did. And I'm glad I saw the Soul Catchers. How many there were – that really shocked me."

"Yes, it shocked us too. And you can be assured it shocked the archangels too. When they first saw it."

"You shouldn't have said that" Reiki said.

POP.

Hadz disappeared.

"Oh, now, it's okay," E-Z said.

"Never mind."

"I still can't figure out what The Furies – Goddesses of Vengeance are getting out of this? What's their endgame? Has anyone figured it out yet?"

"They add more every single day. More children playing games, getting sucked into their web."

"But why isn't there public outcry? Shouldn't we be telling world leaders, Presidents, Prime Ministers? Isn't there anything they could do?"

"Think about it, what's the first thing they'd do? They'd send in the army. More people would die. More Soul Catchers required before their time.

"Gaming from what we've observed is a worldwide phenomenon. The evil sisters are taking the souls of unsuspecting kids."

"But most of the leaders have their own children," E-Z said. "Surely, if they knew they would want to protect their kids and they'd want to protect other kids too."

"More like The Furies – Goddesses of Vengeance would zero in on their kids. It would be like dangling a stick in front of them," Reiki said.

POP.

Hadz was back.

"They'd love it if they could destroy the great and powerful children. Right now, what they seem to be doing is random – chosen within the game" Reiki said.

"Tell me more of what you know about them." E-Z asked.

Hadz whispered, "Their names are Allie, Meg and Tisi. Allie's vengeance is for anger, Meg's is for jealousy and Tisi is known as the avenger."

"Okay, so, why do they smell so bad? And how can the three of them be defeated?" E-Z asked looking at his watch. It was just going on 8 a.m. He needed to talk to the rest of the gang, to get Rosalie back. How was he going to tell them about this terrible trio and all the kids in those Soul Catchers?

"Legend says they were punished for doing their jobs, in the past. Now they've found this loophole with Virtual Reality, a newish human invention." Hadz hesitated. "Why don't humans ever want to live their lives in the now? Why do they have to escape and play stupid games which put their lives in jeopardy?" The wannabe angel was red-faced and extremely cross."

Reiki tried to comfort his friend saying, "They know not what they do."

"Ignorance is no excuse," E-Z said. "We need to send them back to wherever they were before VR was invented. And we need them to return the souls of the children they've taken under false pretenses. Only thing is, HOW are we supposed to convince them that they are doing wrong? That they are stealing lives and punishing people for thoughts, not deeds?

"Now that I've had a glimpse of The Furies – Goddesses of Vengeance - I know we have to help you more than ever. But I still have to convince the others. Even if they do agree, we're still fighting against the odds. I want to be positive. Say we're up to the task. But we won't know for sure, until the time comes to fight."

He punched his pillow and held it on his lap. "Wait a minute, did they die? I mean, did the The Furies – Goddesses of Vengeance escape from their own Soul Catchers? And if they did, how? Who helped them get out?"

Hadz looked at Reiki and Reiki looked and Hadz.

POP.

POP.

They were gone.

"Great!" E-Z said. "Just freaking fantastic!"

CHAPTER 26

BALANCE

ALTHOUGH HE TRIED TO sleep, E-Z could not. He kept thinking asking himself questions. Questions he couldn't answer.

So, he got out of bed and clicked onto his computer and did some digging.

He hit gold before long. When he found a link The Furies – Goddesses of Vengeance and the Three Graces. They seemed to be like the yin and yang of each other. One good one evil. He wondered they could use this information to their advantage. If evil goddesses could be brought to earth, could good goddesses be called back too?

First, before he suggested the archangels bring them back – provided they could do it. He wanted to know exactly what The Graces would bring to the table.

Yes, they were goddesses. The daughters of Zeus who was god of the sky. Their powers were directed to charm, beauty, and creativity. He read on, but couldn't see how they would be much help against The Furies.

Still, he had some time so continued reading He read some text accredited to Nietzsche. His theories about good and evil were still discussed and debated in forums.

Then a memory popped into his head. It was happening less, memories coming back to him about his parents. He hoped they would never stop.

This one was a conversation with his dad. About Newton's Third Law. They'd taken a boat out and were doing some fishing.

"It's how a fish propels himself through the water," his father explained.

Since then, he'd learned more about it from school. He thought Newton and Nietzsche would have had some pretty interesting conversations. But their lives were thousands of years apart.

Then it hit him. He, Lia and Alfred were the polar opposite to The Furies.

Did the archangels already know this? Is that why they seemed so insistent that only he and his team could beat The Furies?

Question that kept running through his mind though was still – could they win?

Was it even possible to stop The Furies?

He had to talk it over with the others.

He turned off his computer, and went back to catch a few zzzs before the other awoke.

Everyone expected him to have all the answers. He didn't have them, but he was doing his best. Since he became leader, life was like that.

CHAPTER 27

RED ROOM

E-Z WAS IN A red room. A room that smelled of blood. The strong iron smell hurt his nose and he covered it with his hand, then walked forward a few steps. His footsteps left marks across the bloody floor. Where was he? In hell? At least he had the ability to run in here, but where to? There were no doors. No windows. No light of any sort and yet, he could see that everything was red. And wet.

He took out his phone and clicked on the flashlight app. Using the flashlight beam he followed the walls all around him. They were all the same. Bloody and dripping. And stinking. He waited. Calling for help didn't seem a smart thing to do. He might be better off it whatever brought him to this place didn't come to meet him. He'd rather not meet them. The flashlight beam switched off and his phone went dead. Afraid to move, he stood stock still and listened.

A crawling, something. Slithering, along the floor. One coming down the wall to the right and another to the left. Three. Snakes.

Then the air in the room shifted, and a familiar smell. Rotting. Eggy. Sulphury. Rotting carcassy.

He covered his nose. As before, it didn't mask the revolting stench.

He waited.

So, they wanted him alone. They had him. He'd make sure they regretted it if it was the last thing he ever did.

"We could eat you for breakfast," Tisi screamed.

"Or lunch," Alli said. "I am a little peckish, after all."

"Or afternoon tea, there's not much of him. Not for three of us to share," Meg said.

E-Z concentrated every fibre of his being on his wings. They were his only hope for escape and they were useless.

"Look!" Meg shrieked. "He's trying to use his ittle-wittle wings."

Tisi and Alli lifted themselves. Meg joined them as they hovered just beyond his reach.

Under his feet, the floor quaked and rumbled. Like it was going to open up and swallow him up. He backed up, to steady himself against the wall. But when he touched it, his shirt felt wet. And when he laid his hand upon it, it came back covered in blood.

"I'm not scared, of you three bitches!" he shouted.

"Maybe you're not frightened of us – yet –" Meg shrieked.

"But you will be very soon," Tisi hissed.

"For now, you can deal with these three," Meg whispered, her foul breath nearly making him vomit.

The three snakes using the leverage of height sprang toward him. Their forked tongues hissing and spitting. Then they started wrapping themselves around each other. Joining, entwining. Until they became one ginormous snake, with three heads and three whips. Whips which snapped in E-Z's direction to hold him in place.

He pushed himself further back. Hearing the squelching blood behind him somehow gave him comfort. His body relaxed as his back sunk into the corner against the bloody dripping wall.

"Look at him," Tisi said. "He's just a boy and he's done no harm to anyone. In fact, he's such a goodie goodie, it's a shame we have to destroy him."

"Yes, his heart is pure," Meg said. "But he has a black spot on his heart. A spot of vengeance he'd like to take against those who were responsible for the deaths of his parents."

"Don't talk about my parents!" E-Z shouted, pushing himself further into the bloody wall. He was afraid. Afraid what they were saying was true. He closed his eyes. If he couldn't see them, then maybe they would go away. Then something behind him gave way. And he went into free fall, backwards. Tumbling. Falling.

THUMP

He landed in his wheelchair, and off they flew.

Back in the Red Room The Furies – Goddesses of Vengeance were furious!

"Go after him!" Tisi shouted.

"Get him!" Meg cried.

"It's too late!" Alli said. "It's like he vanished!"

"Let's get back to Death Valley," Meg said. They left, leaving The Red Room empty. But their stench still lingered.

THUMP.

"You're bleeding," Sam said. "Let's get him into the bathroom. We can see how badly he's hurt." Sam pushed the wheelchair toward the door.

"No, stop!" E-Z said. "I'm okay. The blood is not mine. But I need to get cleaned up. To wash the stench off. Then I'll explain what happened. I promise."

"As long as you're sure you're okay," Sam said.

After he left, Sam, Lia and Alfred couldn't think of anything to say to each other. They waited in silence, for him return.

In the bathroom, E-Z positioned his wheelchair on the ramp. When they rebuilt the house, Uncle Sam invented a new shower for him. It gave him more independence. And it was fun! Similar to a car wash.

He reached up, and put his arms and neck through the straps. He pushed a button so he would move forward, and his chair would follow. Immediately the water began to flow. Cleaning his body and his clothes simultaneously. Every now and then shower gel or shampoo squirted out, followed by water to wash it away.

Now that he was clean, he continued moving forwards and set off the drying mechanism. It dried him and his clothes and made them wrinkle free in minutes.

When he reached the end, he disconnected from the straps, and dropped down into his chair. He checked himself out in the mirror. His hair already looked so good he didn't even have to comb it. He made his way back to his room. When he saw his friends, his stomach lurched, and he vomited.

"I'm sorry," he said. "So sorry."

Lia and Alfred threw their arms around him. They didn't worry about the vomit. Devoted friends don't worry about things like that.

Sam went to fetch a bowl and some water, to clean his nephew up.

E-Z was grateful for the help and it gave him time to think about what he was going to say and how he was going to say it.

"Thanks, Uncle Sam. Uh, what I have to tell you. It's not pretty."

"Go on," Alfred said.

"We're here for you," Lia said.

"Take a seat Uncle Sam."

They listed to everything without saying a word.

"I'm in," Alfred said.

"Me too," Lia said.

"Me three," Sam said.

"Agreed," E-Z said. And a second later, he was on the way back to the white room. Or that's where he hoped he was going.

Anywhere was better than the red room. Anywhere at all.

CHAPTER 28

THE WHITE ROOM

THE WHITE ROOM SEEMED somehow different when his feet touched the ground.

E-Z felt so happy, to be back in the comfort of the white room. Where he could walk around. Touch the books. Smell the books. But something felt strange. Off.

He steadied himself. Noticed his hands were shaking. His knees were trembling. Now his teeth were chattering.

He wrapped his arms around himself wishing he'd brought his jacket. He waited, expecting one to arrive. It didn't.

"What is this place?" he asked.

No answer.

"Cheeseburger, with fries," he said.

Nothing.

"Chop suey, with egg roll," he said, with more authority.

"I demand to know where I am!" he cried.

Nothing.

Nadda.

"Rosalie?" he called. "Are you there? Eriel? Raphael? Anyone? Hadz? Reiki?"

Again nothing.

Not even a polite PFFT to make him relax.

The familiarity of the books were the only anchors holding him in this place. He made his way to the ladder, moved it under the Ds. Expecting to find Charles Dickens he began to climb. Instead, he found that every single book he touched was related to the gaming world.

What the?

And none of the books had wings. They were all brand new. Like no one had opened them before.

He nearly fell off the ladder when a voice said,

"E-Z Dickens – this is not the white room you are familiar with. It's a replica. You've been sent here to research. Every book you require is at your fingertips. Each book must be read and reviewed in full."

"I can't read all of these books quickly; it would take me years to get through all these books!"

"That is why, you will be given an additional power. A power which will only come to fruition within the walls of this room. Read now. Fast. Furious. Memorize it all."

When that voice ended another began,

"Ten, nine, eight, seven, six, five, four, three, two, one. Now, read E-Z Dickens. Get on with it."

E-Z sped through every single book.

When he finished one, another one immediately fell into his hands. Then another, and another.

He read them all, until he could read no more.

He hoped his head wasn't going to explode!

Then he fell against the wall, backed himself into a corner and wept as a plan formulated in his mind.

The idea came to him when he thought of PJ and Arden. Why had The Furies – Goddesses of Vengeance put them into comas instead of Soul Catchers? They were in the game – they played games all the time, why not kill them?

The plan went like this: He and his team would invent their own multiplayer game. Sam would know people who could help in the industry. When The

Furies – Goddesses of Vengeance swooped in to claim their souls – they would take them down.

He wished Arden and PJ were there to play with him – because they would have his back. That was okay, he had their backs. He was going to save them and set them free.

He paced back and forth, thinking it all through. One aspect wouldn't work. If he engaged him in a game, and refused to kill – they'd be on to him. And it might put others in jeopardy.

It's not like he could tell all the game players in the world to stop playing. If he told them the truth, about the three goddesses trying to steal their souls, they'd lock him up.

Still, it was the only idea. The only clear path he could see to beat The Furies – Goddesses of Vengeance in their own game.

Resigned that he could think of anything better, he said, "Get me out of there."

And just like that, he was alone in the real white room with Rosalie and Raphael. He wondered where Eriel was, not that he missed him.

"Okay, I have an idea. A sort of a plan," he said. "But I'm not sure if it will work. I need the answers for two questions. And I have a request for a third – the request is not negotiable."

"Ask away," Raphael said.

"Number one, will I be able to save my best friends PJ and Arden if we face The Furies?"

Raphael hesitated before speaking. "If you succeed, there's no reason why your friends won't be saved."

"Cross your heart?" he said.

She did so.

"As I suspected, their condition is down to The Furies. Is that right?"

"Yes, we believe it to be true. Your friends are lucky in a way because their souls remain intact. What we can't figure out is why, that's if they were targeted by The Furies. In every other case we are aware of, they have taken the souls of children. We know of no others like your friends who remain alive in a comatose state."

"I have an idea about that too, but what I need to know is, if The Furies – Goddesses of Vengeance are defeated what will happen to PJ and Arden? What will happen to all the children whose souls are already in soul catchers? They weren't supposed to die. And what will happen to the homeless souls?"

"Right now, The Furies – Goddesses of Vengeance are using the power of the internet. It gives them access to the hearts and the homes of every person on the planet. It's like you've all left your doors and windows open – so anyone can get in. True there are only three of The Furies – Goddesses of Vengeance – but their powers are great. They are mythical creatures, goddesses whose origins go back to Zeus. You've heard of Zeus, right?"

"I read he was the god of sky and father to The Three Graces. Would they be able to help us, if you brought them back?"

"Zeus is not in this. Nor are his daughters. We archangels don't play around with time. And we always believed that Soul Catchers were sacred. Untouchable. Until now."

"Great, so you think my friends have been targeted by The Furies, but you're not really certain. Not any more than I am, right?"

"Correct. That's because I can't say one hundred percent yes or no. If your friends were playing games. I mean killing within the games...Then they would meet The Furies' criteria.

"But if they wanted them dead – they would already be dead. Unless…no, that wouldn't make sense. It would mean the know about you and your team. There is no way they could know. We've kept it under wraps. If they did know, then they'd be keeping your friends alive in case, they needed leverage."

"You mean as a bargaining chip?"

"Possibly, to be honest I don't know. Like I said, we've kept everything about you and your team under wraps. We, including myself and the other Archangels would do anything to protect you.

"The Furies – Goddesses of Vengeance have been granted powers over the centuries. But they've never targeted innocent children. They've never twisted their agenda to suit their own purposes."

"What are their purposes?" E-Z asked.

"That we don't know."

E-Z said, "That's why we need to have the best chance, to win against them."

"Exactly, but every day they steal more children's souls, and they are speeding up the process."

"Speeding up, by how much?" E-Z asked.

"In the thousands, we think but soon it will be in the millions. Soon it will be too late to stop them."

"Okay, I understand what's at risk here, but we're only kids and we don't want to go in blindly. We're mortal and so are they. We've got to think, consider all options before we risk our lives."

"We understand and like I said we'll have your backs."

"Now on to my next question, I want to know what I am supposed to do with a ten-year-old Charles Dickens?"

"Oh that," Raphael said. "First of all, we had nothing to do with his reincarnation. We have a theory, besides the one we told you, i.e., that you summoned him. We wonder if his return, was a mistake on their part. Perhaps the universe opened up and sent him to help you, as an equilibrium. After all, he is a blood relative. And he's a storyteller, and a plot master. He may have tools and insight you don't yet know of to help you to beat The Furies – Goddesses of Vengeance."

E-Z carefully chose his words. "But he's a kid. He hasn't written a single thing yet. He'll be a distraction and he's from a different time and might put us and our mission in jeopardy."

"It depends," Raphael said. "He could be a secret weapon. He's here, for you. If you believe in him. That he was born to be a writer. Then, at ten years old he will already have all the skills required. Use him to your advantage if you choose to do so."

E-Z clenched his fists. "Are you saying we should use my cousin as bait?"

Raphael laughed and fluttered about, causing an unnecessary breeze.

"It would help if you stopped flapping so much," Rosalie said. "I'm layered with sweaters, still I can't seem to get warm in here. I'd like to go home now, by the way. E-Z and the others have agreed so I've done my bit. Now, so long, farewell. Let me go home."

BINGO.

Rosalie disappeared and landed back in her room. She conversed with Lia in her mind, telling her she'd returned unharmed and was now going to have a nap.

E-Z thought of another non-negotiable requirement.

"I want Hadz and Reiki with me, on our team."

Raphael smiled. "Hadz and Reiki are bound to Eriel by our leader Michael."

"Let me speak to him then. Those two have helped us. They come when I call. If we're going to fight against ancient evil, we need those two on our side to help us."

"Michael is unable to speak with you. However, I will put forth your request. If he deems it necessary, he will let me know and I in turn will let you know. Is there anything else?"

"Yes. I need to know how to be rid of The Furies. Are we meant to kill them? To send them back to wherever they came from? What exactly is it you are asking us to do with these goddesses?"

"Bind them, hold them – and we'll do the rest. If your plan works, then we should be able to take control of the Soul Catchers. We'll reset everything back to the way it was."

"What about those who died, prematurely?"

"All will be equalized...once the enemies have been neutralized."

"Before you send me back," E-Z said, "I need something, some insurance that you're not going to cross us again. Giving us Hadz and Reiki was meant to be that insurance, but since you can't give me that, then I need something else. Something I can take back to the others and say, this is proof they will not renege on us as they have done in the past."

"Like what?"

"Your glasses should do," he said.

Raphael dropped to her knees, her wings ceased flapping and recoiled. "Not that, anything but that," she cried. "Without my glasses I am no help to you and no help to anyone."

"The archangels have held Rosalie here against her will. Used her to get to me. You've changed your minds about promises made, cancelled my trials..."

She touched the rims of her glasses, then removed them. In her hands, the glasses turned into a serpent, a red snake which crawled onto E-Z's arm, and slithered its way up, up, up.

"What the!" E-Z cried, as the serpent continued on up his neck. Over the edge of his chin. It slithered over his tightly closed lips. Up and over his nose. Then it halved itself, and wrapped an end around each of ears. Then returned to its original state pulsating eyeglasses.

"My glasses are yours now, whatever you do – don't let The Furies – Goddesses of Vengeance get them from you. If that happens, then we would all be destroyed."

"Wait!" the voice from the wall said. "What if you fail? After all you're only kids."

"I can't promise success – but we'll give it everything we have. But it would be good to know, if we need your help, that you'll use your powers to help us."

"Deal," the voice boomed.

E-Z was back in his wheelchair in his room with the red glasses pulsating on his face.

"You've got to stop doing that," Uncle Sam said, who was making his nephew's bed. "Before I forget, Sam and I visited PJ and Arden today while we were doing a checkup at the hospital. We ran into PJ's dad; he gave us an update. They're sharing a hospital room now, but neither's condition has changed."

"Thanks, I was going to give them a call. All right everyone, gather round."

CHAPTER 29

WHAT TO DO?

"D O YOU NEED ME to stay?" Sam paused. "Because my wife's waiting for me to massage her feet. The baby is due any day so keeping her waiting is not an option."

"Uh, go ahead and take care of her," E-Z said. "I'll fill you in on the details later."

Lia gave Sam a hug.

"Thanks," Sam said as he closed the door behind him.

The front doorbell sounded.

"I've got it!" Sam called, as he ran toward the front door.

"He's got a lot on his plate," E-Z said.

"It'll be easier, when the baby comes," Lia said.

"It'll be more chaotic," Alfred said. "But let's not worry about that now."

"So, what's the latest?" Lia asked.

"Start with positives if there are any. I sure hope there are some," Alfred said.

"The good news is, I have an idea. The sad news is, I have no idea if it will work against our enemies. They are known as The Furies. Have either of you heard of them? I knew the name from mythology, and they are featured in some games."

Lia shook her head no.

Alfred said, "I've heard of them, but it was a long time ago. Think we read about them in High School, back in the day. I do remember they were evil – three of them maybe? And aren't they goddesses? I have a visual of Medusa in my head. Were they related?"

"They're worse. Much worse because there are three of them," E-Z said. "When I threw up, well, that was straight after my second encounter with them. On the first encounter, it was on a trip with Hadz and Reiki. What they called a little reconnoitering. And don't worry, we were cloaked, but I learned a lot. They've set up headquarters in Death Valley.

"As we suspected, they are targeting kids. In the gaming world. Lia, you asked what their purpose was...It's to push kids over the edge. Kids our age, and even younger.

"Once they get them, their steal their souls. And they put them into Soul Catchers meant for other people. So, when they die, there's nowhere for their souls to go."

"That's so evil!" Lia said.

"So, when the real owners of the Soul Catchers die, what happens to their souls? I mean if their souls have nowhere to go – no home, no heaven – then what happens to them?" Alfred asked.

"That's the thing. They have no eternal resting place – so when they die, they just float around. That's the condensed version anyway. And we need to stop The Furies – Goddesses of Vengeance and we need to stop them soon."

"How are they taking the kids' souls? I don't understand," Lia asked.

"Me either," Alfred said. "Kids, especially kids who play games are very computer savvy. How are they putting themselves in jeopardy? How are The Furies – Goddesses of Vengeance getting access to them in their own homes, right under their parents' noses?"

He thought for a moment, "Are they responsible for PJ and Arden being in comas?"

"Okay, Lia's question first. The Furies – Goddesses of Vengeance punish those who are unpunished – that's been their purpose historically. Their main weapon has always been remorse. They make people feel guilty. To regret doing wrong. And when they do that, they take control. They drive them crazy, make them destroy themselves.

"I told you about the kid who came to my house and tried to shoot me? He said someone in the game told him they'd kill his family if he didn't kill me. They got him to go after me, because of actions he was taking within the game. It took me a hint from Eriel to make that connection. It seemed weird at the time, but it didn't register straight away.

"That's how they do it. A kid is playing a game and to advance in the game, he must kill someone, or even commit mass murder, or, well you get the idea. In the real world, these things are sins and against the law, within the game they are a part of game play. With most games it's the only purpose."

"Wait a minute," Alfred said. "Are you telling me they are punishing kids in the game like they were committing murder in real life?"

"That's right," E-Z said. "That's exactly what they are doing. How they are using the gaming industry to justify – no I don't think that's the right word. I mean to condone their actions in taking the kids' souls."

Lia closed her hands and made them into fists. Then she used them to cover her ears like she didn't want to hear anymore. "You're absolutely right E-Z. We have no choice – we absolutely have got to put a stop to those witches. The sooner the better."

"I know," E-Z said, "but it's not going to be easy. They are goddesses, also known as The Daughters of Darkness and Erinyes. Their number one purpose is to punish the wicked and within the scope of a game – everyone is wicked. It's the only way to advance in the game."

"You said you had a plan, what is it?" Alfred asked.

"First to answer your question about PJ and Arden. My gut feeling is the answer is yes. But I did ask Raphael if she could confirm. She said that she couldn't one hundred percent say one way or the other. Since The Furies – Goddesses of Vengeance had never – to their knowledge – walked away from steal a soul. Not to mention, two souls.

"Oh, one more thing I have to tell you is, in Death Valley, there are thousands of Soul Catchers. Maybe more than thousands and in numbers that are growing every single day. They are as far as the eye can see." He stopped, like his heart was in his throat and wiped a tear away.

"It was difficult to be a witness to it. What they are doing is so premeditated, deliberate. What I can't understand though, is, what's in it for them. I mean, Hadz and Reiki were right in taking me there to see it. If they'd told me, without showing me... it wouldn't have hit me as hard. Oh, and Raphael says they are increasing their intake daily. So, we don't have a lot of time to sit around and think. We need a plan, and we need to take action."

"Are they mortal?" Alfred asked.

"Yes, we're level on that," E-Z said. "So, the plan I thought of was to make a game of our own. Uncle Sam could help. When I'm playing to flaunt kills, then The Furies – Goddesses of Vengeance will come to get me. When they do, we'll trap them and kill them in the game.

"I thought their powers might diminish in the game. But then it occurred to me – what if mine do too."

"We wouldn't know, until it was too late," Alfred said.

"That's right. The more I thought about it, the less effective the idea seemed. Not to mention, if they do have PJ and Arden, stuck in limbo, until their control...Well, they could take their souls away. And we'd lose them."

"You mean it could be a trap?" Lia asked.

"Exactly."

"You've given us a lot to think about," Alfred said. "I think we should sleep on it, mull it over and let's talk about it again tomorrow."

"I'm not sure if I'll be able to sleep," Lia said, "but I agree, let's take a break. I need time to think about how much danger we'll be getting ourselves into. We have to make sure we have each other's backs."

"Sure thing," E-Z said. "Meanwhile, I'll see if I can come up with a Plan B."

Lia left the room and closed the door behind her.

"I wonder who was at the front door?" E-Z asked.

"We can ask Sam in the morning, he's probably still busy attending to his wife's feet."

They laughed."Sounds like a plan," E-Z. "Goodnight Alfred."

"Night E-Z."

CHAPTER 30

OOOH, BABY BABY

"**T**HE BABY IS COMING!" Sam shouted some hours later.

On the way down the hall, he held Samantha's hand in one hand. Slung over his shoulder was an overnight bag. He grabbed the car keys.

"You're not driving, love," Samantha said, putting the keys back down on the counter.

E-Z came out into the hall. "Want us to come with you?"

"I'm fine," Samantha said. "Lia is sound asleep still."

"I'll wake her up and we'll meet you at the hospital, okay?"

Lia glanced over her shoulder, "I've already called a taxi. He's not driving."

Sam smiled, "She's the boss."

"See you soon," E-Z said. "By the way, who was it at the door last night?"

"It was Rosalie. She was exhausted, so we put her in the guest room."

"Okay, thanks," E-Z said.

As he rolled along the corridor to Lia's room, wondering what Rosalie was doing there, he knocked on the door.

"It's me Lia," he said. "Your mom and Uncle Sam are going to the hospital. The baby is coming!"

There was a crash first, then Lia opened the door. The lamp on her night table was on the floor beside the bed. "I'll be ready in second," she said. She closed the door.

He moved along to the guest room. He looked in and Sam was right, Rosalie was fast asleep. He returned to his room, got dressed and tried not to wake up Alfred. Swans weren't allowed in the hospital so waking him would be mean – he'd feel left out. He wrote a note saying Rosalie was sleeping in the guest room and to look after her until they got back. Tell her to make herself at home, he wrote. He left the note so Alfred wouldn't miss it when he woke up.

E-Z closed the door behind him and locked it, then he and Lia got into the waiting taxi and made their way to the hospital.

They followed the signs and soon found the baby ward. Sam was there, pacing up and down like expectant fathers do on television.

"How are you holding up?" E-Z asked.

"How's my mom?" Lia asked.

"Thank you both for coming," Sam said. His hand shook when he attempted to take a drink of water from a bottle. "Samantha is doing really really well. I mean, she's been through it before with you Lia, so she knows what to expect and I'm. Well, I don't know if I can handle it. The course we took, to help us be prepared for today was good – but reality is quite different. I hate hospitals."

"Everyone hates hospitals," E-Z said. "But when they come through those swinging doors. And say you're needed...Then you need to pull it together and get in there and help your wife. Remember you're a team, in this together. You can do this!" He patted his uncle on the back.

"I know."

Lia put her head on Sam's shoulder. "You'll be great."

A nurse arrived. "Your wife needs you. It won't be long now. I'll take you to get scrubbed up, and then you can be with your wife when we take her down."

Sam nodded and off he went.

The last look on his face reminded E-Z of someone standing in front of a firing squad.

"He'll be fine," Lia said, patting E-Z's hand.

Hours later, Sam returned to them with a wide grin across his face. "I have another daughter," he said, "and a son!"

"Two babies?" Lia and E-Z said in unison.

"Yes, two. We only saw one on the scan."

"How's my mom?"

"She's brilliant! Amazing!"

"Can we see her? And the babies?"

"Give them a few minutes, to prepare things. Then you can meet your brother and sister Lia, and E-Z you can meet your cousins."

"Know what you are going to name them yet?" E-Z asked.

"Yes, but we'll tell you together."

"Fair enough," E-Z said.

"Two babies, in that house – with all the others," Lia said.

"I was thinking the same thing. We've already got a full house...but we'll manage. We always do."

They sat together and waited.

EPILOGUE

W EEKS LATER AND IT was January 17th. Christmas had come and gone with all the usual pomp and splendor, same with ringing in the new year. E-Z was another year older, sweet sixteen and the gang was together in his room. Charles Dickens was joining them via Facetime.

Down the hall, the twins – Jack and Jill, were causing a fuss. Sam and Samantha were still getting used the new arrivals' routine. No one in the house had been getting much sleep, until they opened their Christmas gifts. E-Z, Lia and even Alfred received sound blocking headphones.

E-Z had been thinking of other ways they could defeat The Furies. Besides his idea to go after them in game. Few other options were presenting themselves.

While the others were sleeping, he'd had a few conversations with Charles online. Charles thought beating them at their own game would be 'totally badass. '

E-Z was a bit concerned what other phrases those detectorists were teaching Charles. Together they decided to fill the group in on their discussions how to move forward on the gaming idea.

"It's easy," Charles Dickens said. "E-Z and I talked on the phone the other day and we figured out what might work. If they have some intel about The Three – I mean you're all over the internet – they'll know about you. But they won't know about me.

"Not that they'd be afraid of me. Although Edward Bulwer-Lytton once wrote, 'the pen is mightier than the sword.' In this case, I hope it would be true.

"So, I've been practicing with my friends the detectorists. We figure the best game to get them in, is an existing game. And we think we know the perfect game.

"It's called The PK Crew. Game rating is 13+ or 12+ in some places and it's free. The motive of the game is to kill everyone including your family and friends. You're rewarded for each kill, but when you kill people close to you, you even get more points. More cash. Even notoriety within the game. Your picture on PK

TV television. On the front page of the newspaper The Peachy Keen Times. The game happens in a fictional town called Peachy Keen. It's the perfect trap – and it's a game we're going to launch ourselves. I'll play as a twelve-year-old, they'll come into the game and you guys will already be in there."

"It'll be safe enough," E-Z said, "I mean, you're already dead – I mean in your past life - so they can't kill you."

There was a knock on the door, "It's open," E-Z said.

Lia jumped up and threw her arms around Rosalie. "Good to see you're awake," she said as she snuggled into her friend's thick sweater.

Rosalie had become an important part of their team. However, she was only allowed to stay with them for one more day. After that, she had to go back to the home.

As she made her way across the room to sit down, she patted Alfred the swan on the head. They had all become fast friends, since she'd arrived before the babies did.

"I have some things to tell you. First, thanks for making me so welcome. It's been wonderful to see you and thanks for making me feel a part of your team."

"Ahhhhh," Lia said.

"What I need to tell is, I've been writing in a book about other children with special powers like yourselves. It's in my night table drawer. Next time you come to visit, I'll give it to you so you can go and get the others to help you beat The Furies."

"We'll need all the help we can get," Lia said.

"Raphael and Eriel think they can help you, that's why they wanted me to give them details. That's why I wrote it down – so I wouldn't forget anything important."

"Is that why Raphael and Eriel pulled you into the white room?" E-Z inquired.

"Yes and no. I mean yes. They know about the other kids. But no, they didn't outright ask me to hand over the information about them. I know these kids are important to you and without them you can't beat The Furies."

"What do you know about The Furies?" Alfred asked.

Rosalie shivered and crossed her arms. "I know a few things about them. Like, they are three scary sisters, who are back here on earth to do no good."

E-Z said, "You're not kidding. I've seen firsthand the damage they've done so far. We're working on a plan.

But tell us, where are these other kids? Do you think they will help us? That's if we can figure out a way to get them here."

"They are good kids, but you'd have to ask them, and their parents for permission. One is on the other side of the world in Australia, one is in Japan and the other is in the United States in Phoenix, Arizona. There may be others, but these three are the only ones I've had contact with so far," Rosalie said.

"On the other hand, bringing in new kids will complicate things," E-Z said. "Besides, if we fail, then there won't be anyone to take over for us. It might be best for us to manage this ourselves, with the least amount of exposure possible. If we can do it, I mean take The Furies – Goddesses of Vengeance out – why involve others? Strangers? Why risk other kids' lives?"

"It wasn't long ago that we were all strangers," Alfred said.

"I'm still a stranger – even though we're related," Charles Dickens weighed in. "But I'm not one of The Three. E-Z is in charge and I'm happy to do whatever he thinks is best. The detectorists say I'm a newbie. And it's true."

Rosalie looked at the boy in the Screen. "We haven't been introduced properly," she said. "I'm Rosalie and I'm pretty sure I'm more of a newbie than you are."

Charles laughed. "I'm Charles Dickens."

"Any relation to you know, THE Charles Dickens?" Rosalie asked.

"Uh, yes, I'm him – reincarnated."

Rosalie laughed. "I thought I'd heard everything. Well, I'm happy to meet you Charles."

There was a loud knock on the front door.

A few seconds later, booted feet made their way along the hallway against Sam's protests.

"Rosalie," the burliest of the two men said through the closed door. "It's time to return to the home. You need your medicines, so come on out, or we'll have to come in for you."

Rosalie stood, "Looks like I told you everything you need to know and in the nick of time." She walked to the door, opened it, and left with the attendants.

In the back of the ambulance, one minute, then in the white room. The shelves and the books were the same, but the smell wasn't. Before there wasn't a smell, but now, it was bad. Stinky. Nasty. Like bleach and rotten eggs.

Through the wall, three women dressed from head to toe in black entered. Instead of hair, they had snakes. And more snakes crawled up and down their arms. They flew at her. Their bat-like wings contrasted with the purity and whiteness of the room. Blood foamed out of their eyes, as they flicked their whips in her direction.

And their stench was unbearable.

"Tell us what we want to know," The Furies–Goddesses of Vengeance chided in unison.

"I don't know what you are asking me," Rosalie said, holding her nose.

WHIP.

The crack of the whip grazed the skin on the old woman's cheek. When she touched her face, and looked at her hand it was covered in blood.

"You know," Allie said, while she and her sisters flicked their whips in the vicinity of the older woman once again.

"I don't know what you mean."

A bookshelf toppled over. If it hadn't been for the fast-moving ladder, Rosalie would have been crushed under it.

WHIP.

I'm dreaming, Rosalie thought. I need to wake up. I need to wake up NOW and get away from these horrible stinky creatures.

Another bookshelf fell.

Then another. And another.

Soon, the ladder also hit the floor and bounced. Once, twice, three times. Then shattered into pieces.

"Oh no!" Rosalie cried.

"You'll tell us love," Tisi demanded, as she lifted the older woman off the ground as her snaked arms wrapped around her.

Rosalie's feet dangled precariously. While the snakes tightened their grips around her upper body.

"Watch it, sister, you'll give her a heart attack," Meg screeched moving closer to Rosalie. "Give us what we want love."

"I'm not telling you, anything. No matter what you do to me," Rosalie said.

She was being so brave. For she knew she wasn't alone. Lia was there, listening.

"This is a complete waste of time," Allie said as she sent a whip into the air and struck down an entire wall of bookshelves. A few winged books struggled to get out from under the shelves. One tried to fly with its only remaining wing.

Tisi turned toward the far wall and set the books burning. They fell, like dominoes, on top of poor Rosalie who was buried under the burning books.

The Furies – Goddesses of Vengeance laughed loud and proud.

Rosalie called Lia's name in her mind. Where are you Lia? she asked. Where are you little one?

Back at the house, E-Z opened his laptop. "Okay, we've had the chance to sleep on it. Are we all in agreement, that we have no choice but to fight The Furies – Goddesses of Vengeance?"

Lia and Alfred nodded.

"And we need to get these other kids and bring them here. There are three of us and three of them. Lia, you go to Phoenix – Little Dorrit can take you or you can fly in a plane."

"I prefer Little Dorrit."

"Okay, first kid is sorted. Although we don't know her name or where exactly she is in Phoenix, Arizona. And you'll need to clear it with her parents. It won't be easy as you'll have to let them know what kind of danger their child will be getting into."

"Yeah, I'll have to get more details from Rosalie."

"Alfred, you can go to Japan. I suggest you fly – we'll have to work out logistics. You'll need to fly back with the kid that's assuming his parents will give you the go ahead. Again, we need specifics from Rosalie where the kid is. And there will be a language barrier, unless you know Japanese?"

Alfred shook his head.

"I'll get a translator."

"We'll get you a phone and you can put an app on which would do the translating for you. There'll be a learning curve," E-Z said. "Especially since you don't have fingers."

"Sounds good to me," Alfred said. "I'll have to start working with the phone pronto. It shouldn't take long to figure it out. In the meantime, Rosalie can tell the child that I'm a swan – so they won't fall over and faint when they first see me."

"That's a good idea," Lia said. "But how are you going to type?"

"I can use my beak."

"Or a voice activated program," E-Z said.

"Cool," Lia and Alfred said in unison.

"And I'll fly to Australia. I'll catch a plane back with the kid, but it'll be quicker if I go directly there. Oh, and one more thing, we need to think of a trapdoor for ourselves. Someway we can get out – in the event of one or more of us being caught or killed or getting hurt. We must be prepared for everything. If we die before we finish this thing, there'll be no one left to pick up the pieces."

"The archangels," Lia stammered, then stopped. She shivered, then she couldn't catch her breath. She wrapped her arms around herself.

"Are you okay?" E-Z asked.

"Shhh," she said. There were no sounds in the room nor in her mind, there was absolute and complete silence. Her heart rate returned to normal as did her breathing.

"False alarm," she said. "I thought something was wrong, like I was getting an SOS, but everything seems fine now."

"Does that happen often?" Alfred inquired.

"No," Lia said.

"Okay, let's start brainstorming," E-Z said. And they spent the rest of the day making a list, zeroing in on what could go wrong and what could go right.

They went to their rooms and slept.

It was a peaceful night for everyone but Rosalie.

Rosalie, whose voice was not heard.

Whose voice was not answered.

No help arrived.

The White Room was destroyed.

No one came to save Rosalie.

From the wicked Furies.

Thank you!

Dear readers,

Thank you for reading the third book in the E-Z Dickens Series...I'm sorry about the sad ending but sometimes these things happen.

The final book is available now!

Thank you once again to all the folks who helped me to make this series everything it could be such as my beta readers, proof readers and editors. Kudos!

To my friends and family, thanks for your encouragement and support.

And as always, Happy Reading!

Cathy

About The Author

Cathy McGough is a Canadian author whose work spans children's literature; young adult fiction; literary fiction; psychological thrillers; poetry; short stories and non-fiction. She lives and writes in Ontario, Canada with her family.

Also By:

YA

E-Z Dickens Superhero Book Four: On Ice

A Mathematical State of Grace Complete Series

NON-FICTION

103 Fundraising Ideas For Parent Volunteers With Schools and Teams (3RD PLACE BEST REFERENCE 2016 METAMORPH PUBLISHING)

+ Children's Books